Mrs Austin

P[...]
T[...]RE

CW00867092

PENGUIN THEATRE

VERONICA HELEY

Scripture Union
130 City Road, London EC1V 2NJ.

By the same author
Swift Books
Sky High

Leopard Books
Hawkeye of Paradise Row
The Paradise Row Gang
Hawkeye hits the Jackpot

Tiger Books
Good for Kate!
Dancing Feet

For 6–8s
Natasha's Badge
Natasha's Swing
Natasha the Brownie

© Veronica Heley 1992
First published 1992

ISBN 0 86201 736 X

Phototypeset by Intype, London
Printed and bound in Great Britain by Cox and Wyman Ltd,
Reading

To Sarah Miller, who gave me the information on which this book is based, and whose courage I admire greatly.

To The British Dyslexia Association, 98 London Rd., Reading RG1 5AU, whose helpline is always open on 0734–668–271.

To Society Expeditions, Albany House, Suite 301, 324–6 Regent St., London W1R 5AA, who arranged Sam's voyage to Antarctica.

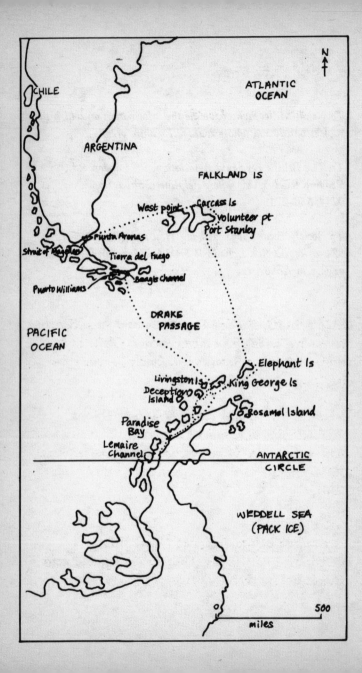

N

CHILE

ATLANTIC
OCEAN

ARGENTINA

FALKLAND IS

West point   Carcass Is
              volunteer pt
Punta Arenas   Port Stanley
Strait of Magellan
      Tierra del Fuego
            Beagle channel
Puerto Williams

DRAKE
PASSAGE

PACIFIC
OCEAN

                    Elephant Is
          Livingston Is
Deception   King George Is
Island
              Bosamel Island
Paradise
Bay
Lemaire
Channel   ANTARCTIC
                     CIRCLE

                    WEDDELL SEA
                    (PACK ICE)

                              500
                     miles

1

SAM'S LOG, *star date Dec 09, on bord the ss Society Adventurer, sailing from Punta Arenas, Chile. My mishun, to explore Antarctica, to boldly go where few have gone before. Weather clowdy.*

Embarked at 1500 after boring flight from London.
1700 checked in at reseption. Tea.
1830 in the lounge for introduction to staff and lecturers.
1930 Dinner.
2230 set sail.

This book belongs to Samantha (Sam) Ward,
10 Brookvale Rd., Ealing, London. I'm eighteen years old, and just left skool.

This is Sam's alternative log.

Talking into a tape recorder is ten times better than trying to commit my inmost to paper.

Some days I can write without any mistakes. Other days I can't even read back what I've written. So, this tape recorder wasn't a bad idea.

The parents'll be happy enough with a short daily log in my exercise book. They don't mind if I spell Antarctica with two ks, and I don't mind making the effort for them, because they'll never get to see penguins outside of a zoo.

This second, private record is just for me.

My friend Luke suggested it. He said I was to borrow his tape recorder and talk into it, whenever I could. I thought he meant he wanted a more detailed log about my trip to Antarctica. After all, it isn't only the parents who won't get to see penguins in their natural surroundings. He said, yes, he'd be interested in that, but what he really thought I should do was talk about my problems.

I suppose he means my dyslexia.

OK, so let's deal with that. I'm dyslexic, but as far as I'm concerned, now that I've left school it's no problem. I know how to deal with it. I *have* dealt with it. I've come out with good enough A levels to go into accountancy. So what have I got to worry about?

What it is with Luke, he's always got to prod away, trying to find out what makes people tick. If the onion didn't have skins to take off, he'd invent them.

Well, I'm not like an onion. I don't need to hide things. What you see, is all there is. I'm OK. I know Luke thinks I've got choices to make, and maybe even secrets to hide, but I haven't. And if I do have nightmares, well, everyone gets nightmares, don't they, and I don't see why he should get worked up about it.

Anyway, a fortnight away from everything will put me right.

So, here begins my log.

This is Sam Ward speaking, of Ealing, West London. Ealing is a nice enough place to live. I'm eighteen years old, and have just left school with two A levels. They call me a big girl when they want to be nice to me. And they'd better not let me hear them calling me anything else!

Good Points: blondish thick hair, totally out of control unless I keep it short. Blue eyes. Fair skin which is no problem at the moment. Wearing dungarees, sweat shirt and boots.

Likes: the theatre, books, penguins.

Dislikes: school, stupid people, Brussels sprouts.

Educated: sort of.

Friends: a couple, three if you count Kate (which I don't, always). Luke, of course. Rocco, that's short for Morocco, which is a nickname.

Family: the usual parents, OKish, quite caring really, but not exactly the brightest.

Career: accountancy, all taken care of.

Ambition: Don't know. Millions of things I don't want to do. I'd prefer not to work in an office, though I suppose I'll have to. They'd better not ask me to teach . . . well, I couldn't anyway, could I? There's loads of things I can't do.

If there is a God, why did he make me like this?

Scrub that bit, it's irrelevant.

The flight was OK. Just like any other flight. Even Punta Arenas airport looks much like any other airport, except for the backdrop of the mountains. And being so small. More like a bus station than an airport.

This boat, now, is something else. Luxury on the waves. This must be what those old-fashioned cruises were like. It's a different world from dear old Ealing. Different smells, sounds, voices, colours . . .

From an English winter I've jumped to the tip of South America and now I'm heading into an Antarctic summer. Topsy turvy land.

I think I know what to expect. There'll be ice and snow, boiling water from volcanic activity, seals and cape pigeons, whales . . . and penguins. I'm really looking forward to the penguins. I've got a fixation on penguins. They're so cute!

Outside, there's a clear hard grey light, a swelling grey sea, seagulls and all that stuff. It could be somewhere off the north coast of Scotland, only it isn't. It's umpteen degrees south and heading for bad weather, if I'm any judge of the matter.

I'm a good sailor. I hope the woman sharing my cabin is a good sailor, too. All the other passengers are having coffee after dinner, chatting with the tour leaders and tame lecturers they've got on board to keep us happy if the weather turns foul. Swapping put-down stories . . . you know, how much more I paid for my second home or camera than you did! Most of them are over sixty. The woman I'm sharing with looks like a tough type of maiden aunt, probably here to wait on aged parents. Being cooped up with that lot is going to be a real drag.

10

I'd wanted to go solo, but the parents insisted I join a guided tour.

I've been reading up about this part of the world for ever.

Whales, dolphins, albatrosses! There's to be a champagne prize for the first one to spot an iceberg, not that we're far enough south for icebergs yet.

One good thing, the rest of them probably won't want to be out on deck in all weathers, as I intend to be.

I don't know how I'm going to fill up the rest of this tape. Luke said this was my last chance to get myself sorted out. What for, I ask myself? I know what I'm doing. He may not like the idea of my becoming an accountant, sorting out other people's problems, but what's that got to do with it? It's what I've planned to do since I was knee high. I don't understand . . . !

Sometimes, I think Luke really enjoys being the odd man out. He makes a sort of career out of being different. He likes to tell other people what to do with their lives. I suppose that's part of his wanting to be a doctor. That, and going to church. It's not all a pose, though. I thought it was, at first. But he actually believes in God and all that guff. I know what the words are supposed to mean, but . . .

Well, that's all for now. They said there'd be a late night snack served in one of the lounges, and I suppose I might as well see what they've got. One thing; their food's really good. Over and out.

Dec 10 at sea en roote to the Falkland Islands.
  Weather: Partly clowdy (cloudy?) SW winds.

*Copied from log issued to all passengers: A fresh Atlantic
breeze greeted us as we cleared Magellan Strait mid
morning, setting our course towards the Falkland
Islands. Captain's Welcome Cocktail and Dinner in
the evening.*

'A fresh Atlantic breeze,' my foot. Half a gale, in my
terminology. It's freezing cold out. Nothing to be seen
except waves. Why did I come? The other passengers
are like I said; much older, retired people mostly, with
thousands to spend on their holidays. It makes you want
to puke.

The woman I'm sharing with is not bad. She's ginger-
haired . . . no, make that auburn haired, because I'm
sure she thinks it's auburn and not ginger . . . anyway,
she's much older than me, late thirties, maybe early fort-
ies. She's some kind of journalist, or editor or something
for small house magazines. Freelance. She's got a camera
I'd give my eye teeth for, and she's on some kind of
photographic mission to capture penguins for posterity.

I knew I'd like her when I heard about the penguins.
She's too busy to talk to me, though. She thinks I'm just
a schoolkid still. I don't blame her. I did make a crashing
entry into the saloon for supper. Brought a whole table-
cloth of stuff down with me. Just my luck.

Perhaps when I'm older, I can be like her. I always
wanted to be a reporter, fly to fires, cross-question

crooks and all that. Impress MPs.

I'm babbling. Fat chance.

The weather's getting worse. They're all in the saloon, playing cards and listening to the lecturers who are frightfully high-powered. You can see them, the lecturers, I mean, wondering what on earth this lumpy schoolgirl is doing on their cruise. A couple of them are dropping off for a stint in one of the Antarctic camps. They've nothing to say to me, or I to them, so I'm going to be a good girl and do as Luke says. Get it all down on tape. Start at the beginning.

Well, we'll skip birth pangs and playgroup and first school and all that aggro. 'Clumsy girl, can't you look where you're going . . . look what you've done now . . . oh really, Samantha, can't you do the simplest little thing without making a mess of it?'

Forget all that. It doesn't count. I got through it, somehow. There was only one teacher I'd ever want to remember in my prayers – that is, if I did pray, which I don't. Now she was nice. I mean, she got upset when I couldn't cope. Talked to me, listened to me, and didn't get mad even when I hit her.

Yeah, I'd forgotten that. I did hit her. Shame! It makes me feel sick to think of it, because she was only trying to help. But that other teacher . . . what was her name? . . . used to frighten the daylights out of me, shouting at me, her mouth getting larger and larger . . . looming over me like a great black . . . ugh!

Well, she's probably dead by now. And when I got into the next teacher's class, things did get better. She got me extra reading, and did five minutes each day with me on my tables, and if I had to drop my music lessons, it was worth it to keep up in class.

I wonder where she is now. Someone said she went on to be deputy head somewhere. I wonder what she'd say if she knew I came out with two A levels. I bet she'd be pleased.

So skip school and Dad changing jobs, and Mum getting a part-time job and all that. The other kids left me alone at school after they found out it wasn't safe to laugh at me. Maybe I ought to put this bit in, though I'm not proud of it. Luke would frown if he knew, but in those days if anyone laughed at me I used to bite them! Well, not hard, of course, but . . .

I used to get into a lot of trouble for that. I can't remember much else about those days except . . . no, it's gone. I think . . . was I afraid of the dark? Mum bought me a special lamp with a low-wattage bulb. I had that for years, though I don't think I used it much. It was just there, in case I needed it.

The others didn't try teasing me at High School. Quite a few of my class from the old school came on with me, and I was much bigger than them, anyway, so I could see the word getting round . . . don't trouble Trouble, or she'll trouble you.

Meaning me, Samantha Ward. Only I got them to call me Sam pretty quickly, and that was when I made Mum have my hair cut short. She was always on at me to dress nicely, and have my hair permed or something. Fat chance. Jeans and T-shirts. Dungarees and sweat shirts. Trainers. Bovver boots. And I cut my hair with the big shears till she saw I meant it, and let me have it done properly.

That felt better.

No sports, though. Dad was always going on about that, but I think Mum understood. She's a bit cack-handed herself.

It's not true that I can't tell my left from my right – I can, especially with my new gloves, which have an L and an R embroidered on the backs – but I do get Mum to mark my shoes and boots. Digital watches are a boon. The times I used to get muddled with the old sort!

So, High School. An awful struggle to keep in the top sets for everything, and beginning to get bored with having to work so hard. I mean, other people didn't have to. Like Kate. Not only did she look like something off the cover of a magazine, but she kept scraping into the top sets for everything without even trying. I swore blind she got the boys to help her with her homework, but I don't think they did, not really.

I didn't want to be like her, of course. All she ever thought about was boys and makeup and not laddering her tights and how short she could get away with wearing her skirts. Yuk. Boys are so stupid, always falling for that type. Even Luke.

Yes, even Luke, and he ought to have known better . . .

Shall I delete that bit? If Luke hears it, he'll know I'm jealous.

I can easily delete it. Come to think of it, I don't really want Luke to hear all this. There's other bits I've put in which I wouldn't want broadcast to all and sundry.

Well, I can keep the tape private, if I want to. There's nothing to say I have to turn it over to Luke when I get back.

So let's have a new heading.

THE DAY WE MET. Sounds like Mills and Boon! Well, Kate would think in those terms, wouldn't she? The day Kate met her heart throb, the adorable Luke, and how she walked off with him even though he could see I was in trouble.

I have to admit that Kate is pretty. She always was, even when we were in playgroup together. She looks Irish, though she hasn't got any Irish blood in her that I know of. She's all dark curly hair and eyes, a clear skin, and a pretty, breathy voice. From the age of eight she had the boys carrying her lunch box for her. Whereas I got all the bumps and fights, and clowned about, making believe I didn't care, she just used to sit there, not quite smiling, and everyone would try to sit next to her. Teacher's pet.

I used to say there was a sign reading 'vacant' between her eyes, but the others didn't like me any the better for saying it. She never threw tantrums like me, or swore. I used to play awful tricks on her, like putting crisps down the tops of her boots. She hated that. It was so funny, to see her hopping about . . .

She just got up my wick, that's all.

Anyway, we went through to High School together, and would you believe we ended up in the same sets, mostly. It would have been nice to have got away from her, and I don't know how she did it, because I had to slog away at my homework for hours and hours while she never seemed to do any. She was always out with friends or playing tennis or something. But there she was, swanning along in the top sets for English and Maths with me, and then she went and plumped for Drama as well, just as I was wondering whether I'd dare go in for it. I suppose I ought to have realised that she'd go for Drama. She always got the good parts in the middle school plays, while I was a tree or something equally stupid.

I want to get this clear. We were not friends. We just knew each other from way back.

So we come to the Worst Time of My Life. (Well, the accident was worse, I suppose, but that was physical, whereas this was Mental Anguish of the First Water).

I hadn't told anyone at school about Dad losing his job. Being made redundant, rather. Lots of people were being made redundant at that time, but I couldn't bear people at school acting sympathetic, so I didn't say anything. I suppose I was even clowning around more than usual.

It would have to be old Snowcem taking English that day.

'You, girl, what's your name, Ward? Stand up, and show me your hands!'

I'd got chewing gum in my hand, nicely softened after five minutes in my mouth. The gum was wrapped around a pellet of paper, and I'd been flicking the pellets up to the ceiling, where they clung right over old Snowcem's head. I was sure he hadn't noticed anything because I'd been careful with my timing.

But there he was, glaring at me. 'Well, girl, I'm waiting.'

I stood up, carefully scraping the chewing gum pellet off on the underside of the table as I did so.

'What, me, Mr. Snow?'

'Yes, you, girl. Show me your hands.'

I held them out. Clean, of course. He stood over me, peering at my hands, but didn't spot the chewing gum. He had a long thin neck with curving black hairs on it, rather like a vulture. His neck was red, too, in the winter. He should have retired years ago, because he'd been at the school for yonks, but his sort, the sarcastic sort, never seem to take early retirement, do they? He took the second set for English, so we didn't usually have anything to do with him.

He picked up my exercise book and flicked through a couple of pages. I began to whistle, more or less silently. I'd done my homework after a fashion, but what with the scene the night before after my father broke the bad news, and then mother trying to be brave while leaking tears around the edges, I can't say the pages did me credit.

'Disgraceful!' he said, rolling his rrrs.

Little did he know that my work is a miracle of neatness compared to what it used to be. Why, in the old days I used to write my 'b's and 'd's back to front, not to mention my 'p's and 'q's. I might have told him that if he hadn't been so worked up, but as it was, I decided to let it pass. He took the book to the front of the class, and held it up for them to see. 'Just look at this! Slipshod! Appalling handwriting! And as for the spelling, I can honestly say I've seen better in an infants' class.'

Some of the class snickered. Kate was smoothing over the edge of a fingernail with a worried look on her face. A snagged fingernail could occupy her mind for hours.

Mr Snow flapped his extraordinarily large elbows, like a rooster preparing to crow.

'As you are no doubt aware, your form teacher Mr Toft had an accident in his car on the way home last night. We heard at breaktime that he will be kept in hospital for some weeks. Consequently, I shall be taking his top set for English right through to the summer holidays.

'Now I came prepared to impart a modicum of under-standing of T. S. Eliot's poetry to an intelligent and mature set of students. And what happens? I find myself reduced to teaching a disruptive infant how to spell CAT.' He glared at me. 'Can you spell cat, girl? Repeat after me. C, A, T.'

I realised then that he must have spotted the pellets on the ceiling, and was going to take it out of me.

Kate's hand went up. Bad timing, if she wanted to keep in his good books. And I bet she only wanted to go to the loo so that she could deal with her fingernail.

'Please, Mr. Snow. I think Samantha's dyslexic.'

Dyslexic? What was that? I hadn't heard the word before.

'Dyslexic?' Snowcem made a meal of the word, swooping from high to low and back again. 'And just what do you imagine that word means, eh? Perhaps you think it can be trotted out to excuse sloppy, careless work. Well, my girl, that won't wash with me. And why not? I'll tell you why not. Because the word 'dyslexia' is a meaningless term, coined by people who have never taught a class in their lives. I have been teaching for forty-one years, and I tell you that dyslexia does not exist. What does exist is laziness, and carelessness, and downright stupidity . . . none of which have any place in the top set for English. Do I make myself clear?'

He slapped the book back down in front of me, and bared his yellowing teeth in a grin.

I could feel the blood rush up through my neck and into my face. I tried not to let him see how upset I was. He couldn't really be saying that I had to drop out of the top set for English, could he?

Being in the top set for English was the best thing about school.

'Well, girl? What have you to say for yourself? Nothing? I thought not. I'll have a word with the Deputy Head and get you moved to a more suitable place . . . the remedial class, for instance. And now perhaps the rest of us can get on with the study of literature.'

I was just about to explode when the bell went. I knocked my book onto the floor, and the new boy picked it up.

2

Sam's log: official.

Dec 11 CARCASS ISLAND, *Falklands Arr 0800*
Dep 1300
  Weather: clowdy/drizzle, W winds

Walked along the bay. Saw lost of plants and wildlife.
Visited gentoo and magellanic penguin rookeries. We
were fed at the Mc Gill settlement (and how!) Reboarded
at Pattison cove.
N.B. They call the ship-to-shore boats a weird name:
'Zodiacs'. Crazy. The Zodiacs are about 4m long and
go anywhere, very fast. At spede the bow lifts out of
the water and you're smothered in spray.

WEST POINT ISLAND Arr 1400 Dep 2000
Weather: o'cast/rain, W'ly winds

*Tricky manoovre into the narrow mouth of Hope
Harbour. Anchored off Napier settlement. The boat
sent food ashore, and the Napier people all joined in..
The food is disgustingly good, and there's so much of
it! Uphil hike to rockhopper penguin and black-browed
albatross colony among extrordinary tussock grass,
growing chest high or higher. We're supposed to keep
the length of a Zodiac away from all wild life, but I
was trying to see ovar one of thse tussocks, and I parted
the grass and I was looking right down on a rockhopper
on its nest! I don't know who was most surprised! But
he didn't run, and niether did I. We looked at one
another for quite a while, and he must have known I
wasn't going to hurt him, because he just stuck there,
with his head twisted round, looking at me. Close to,
there's a marvellous sheen to them. Purple plum black.
I wanted to reach out and touch, but I didn't. He was
so . . . clean!*

    *N.B. Rockhoppers are my favorites! They have tufted
crests which make them look comical. The best day
yet!!!*

Hi, this is me, recording my private log. I went on both
trips ashore. After we got back I was full of what we'd
seen, but *not* ready to sit still and listen to another
lecture . . . what do they think we are, school kids or

something? They lecture us uphill and down dale. I suppose it's to give us 'value for money'. If you can't go ashore, take a lecture. If you're bored, take a lecture. If you want to drop off to sleep . . . well, you get the idea. I don't want to go to sleep. I had the nightmare again last night, and the last thing I want to do is to go back to sleep.

The nightmare is something I ought to talk about, I suppose. But when you've just had it, the last thing you want to do is talk about it. That way you bring it all back.

So let's talk about something else. I've been up on the Obs deck, but there was nothing much to see except rain, and it was cold, so I suppose I might as well get on with this recording lark.

The most painful period of my life. Old Snowcem chucking me out of the top set.

Luke picked up my book and put it on the desk, while everyone else in the class did their usual lemming dive for the door.

Luke was a strange-looking kid. Tall, thin, black curls like Kate's. Blue eyes like Kate's. No, not like Kate's, because he looked intelligent, and the only thing that brought a sparkle to her eyes was being admired, preferably by someone of the opposite sex.

There was a silvery flash to Luke's eyes which made him look intense. He said, 'How come you're in the top set for English, if you're dyslexic?'

I didn't want to admit my ignorance, so I fudged it.

'Yeah, well. I dunno. Mr Toft looks at things differently from old Snowcem.'

Kate came up, teasing out one of her curls. She spoke to me, but her eyes were on the new boy. 'Samantha, you mustn't let Mr Snow get away with it. You must go to the Deputy Head and get it sorted.' And to Luke, 'Hi, I'm Kate, and this is Samantha. We usually eat together. Would you like to join us?'

She really does talk like that, all toffee and good manners. The parents think she's terrific. It comes of her having a father nearly old enough to be her grandfather, or something.

Anyway, I could see this combination of sweet talk and good looks was having its usual effect upon the audience. I tried to put the record straight by saying my name was Sam, not Samantha, but Rocco came bumbling up, and no-one took any notice.

Kate introduced him as well. '..and this is Rocco, short for Morocco, because he comes from the Middle East, though not actually from Morocco, but . . .'

'Libya,' said Rocco, grinning at Luke.

My book had a dirty footprint on it. If anything made me feel vicious, it was getting my books in a mess. Books were sacred. People were expendable.

They seemed to be waiting for me to make a move, and everyone else in the class had gone by that time, so I told them, 'I've got something to do. You go on ahead and I'll join you.' I couldn't bear their chatter. I began to whistle. I was a born whistler, a regular don't care girl.

My gran – she's dead now – used to say, 'Don't care was made to care!'

I'd care all right, if Snowcem went through with his

threat. But I wasn't going to let anyone see that I was upset. 'I care for nobody, no, not I, and nobody cares for me . . .'

I waited for Snowcem – for *Mister* Snow – after school, and tried an apology on for size. He treated me to one of his crocodile grins. You could see he enjoyed chewing people up.

Apparently Snowcem didn't like 'immature, trouble-making children'. His exact words.

Furthermore, he said it wouldn't be any use my com-plaining to the Deputy Head, because my behaviour had already been discussed at top level. He said I'd been warned several times about playing practical jokes in school, and about neatness and spelling.

Of course I'd been warned, but no-one expects to be shot from top to bottom of the ladder because of a few bits of paper and some chewing gum, do they?

He told me I was to report next day to Miss Grey – Earl Grey, they call her – for English. Since Snowcem was being upped to take the first set, she was taking the second set, which meant her class would scrape through their exams with a D or an E. I'd almost rather it was the remedial class. Earl Grey was hopeless, everyone knew it. No-one worked in her class, and she couldn't keep order, either.

I didn't know what to do about it, apart from blowing up the school. I felt like hitting darling Snowcem. I think he saw that in my eye, for he removed himself into the staff room sharpish. I stood there quite a long time, grinding my teeth. I couldn't go home and add to all the trouble there. I needed space in which to be someone else for a change, someone who didn't make stupid mistakes and mess things up. So I went to Drama Club.

I'd only joined a couple of weeks before. Kate had joined some time back, and was already getting small parts. Her presence wasn't a plus from my point of view, but since I wasn't aiming for the footlights, it didn't put me off entirely.

What it was, I had this hankering for backstage work. I hadn't let on because Kate and the others would only have laughed at me.

I felt better as soon as I smelled the special kind of dust that settles around lights in a theatre.

I had another good reason for going to Drama Club. I had my eye on the A.S.M.'s job. They'd appointed some fool of a fourth year boy as Stage Manager, and he was making a right mess of it. He'd put me on curtains and props, but I'd kept my eyes open and worked out what he was supposed to be doing, even though half the time he was round the back having a quick fag, which was criminally stupid with all that flammable stuff around.

While he was messing things up, I was doing his job, and that did my ego no harm at all, I can tell you. Even our Drama Teacher, Mrs Whittle, was beginning to get the message, and to give me the odd smile now and then.

I love backstage at the theatre. The heavy shadows, whose shape you can alter with a flick of a switch, the brilliance of the lights, and the warmth, and watching the actors make fools of themselves. Most schoolkids can't act for toffee, and those that can usually go way over the top. But we had a sixth year girl who could curl your toes laughing just by bouncing onto the stage, and a wimp of a third year whom you wouldn't suspect of being up to stealing fags from the corner newsagents, who had a voice like a buzz saw and could milk tears from a stone. Now that's what I call a gift. I watched them as if I were a video camera, recording it all for posterity.

Even feeling as frantic as I did that day, the old magic still worked. I wished I could always live in a theatre. Perhaps I'd turn into another Phantom of the Opera, and live under the stage and pop out from one of the trap-doors and scare people silly.

I tried not to think about the future while I checked props and gave the lighting cues. (Our so-called A.S.M. was nowhere to be seen, as usual). It was beginning to dawn on me that I hadn't got a future if I weren't allowed to stay in the top set for English. I wasn't marvellous at any subject, but I got by with a lot of hard work. Only I needed good grades in five subjects to go on to do accountancy, which was what I was aiming for.

I felt sick. When the rehearsal was over, I thought of asking Mrs Whittle to intercede with Snowcem for me, but if he'd taken over as Head of Department, it wouldn't do any good.

I told myself not to panic. There was a way out, and somehow I'd find it. I got on my bike and rode off home.

Then, Shock! Horror! Turning into our road, Rocco walked out in front of me, and I nearly knocked him over.

'Idiot!'

He wasn't listening.

He had the blank, glazed look of someone in shock. I got a hold of his anorak and led him back onto the pavement. My bike was all right. Luckily. I'd have killed him if it hadn't been.

He pulled away from me and started to walk back into the traffic. Really, some people are so stupid, you wonder why they're let out alone.

I yanked him back onto the pavement, and spun him round. He didn't recognise me. This on top of everything else! I looked around for a friendly face or a neighbour, or someone who could be trusted to ring for an ambulance. No-one. Any time you don't want a neighbour breathing down your neck about riding on the pavement or whatever, they're out in droves. Today, zilch.

Keeping hold of his arm and pushing my bike, I steered him along the pavement. He lived not far from me, on the opposite side of the road. He was quite docile. It was rather like taking a dog for a walk on a lead.

Then he stopped, and went all stiff. I couldn't get him to move on, so I stopped, too.

'Sam?' he said. 'What you doing?'

'Trying to stop you committing suicide, you dum-dum. What's the matter with you?'

'Oh, didn't I say? Parents. Phone call. Just now. My parents, back home. Killed. The bombing.'

He went on staring at me with those full round eyes of his. I felt awful. I mean, what can you say to someone when they come out with that sort of thing?

I said, 'I thought they'd been bombed out before, and

were all right, living with cousins or something.'

'That's right. Our old house was being repaired. It was almost finished. My mother told me they were going to move back in at the weekend. Only, they won't be able to now, will they?'

'No, I suppose not.' It was ironic, really. His parents had gone to live in the house belonging to one of their numerous brothers, which was vacant because said brother and his family were currently living here in England, across the road from us. Rocco's uncle had some sort of diplomatic job. He'd wanted his kids to get an English education and had volunteered to house and feed and water Rocco – who was his nephew, of course – while Rocco was getting educated.

Rocco's mum was a British citizen, so Rocco had a British passport, and could stay on and get his education free, but his little cousins were all at fee-paying schools. I supposed it wouldn't make much difference to Rocco's education that his parents were dead, but that isn't the kind of thing you can tell a boy to be thankful for just after the worst has happened.

I fidgeted a bit, not knowing how to deal with this. 'Do you want to come back home with me? Mum ought to be back by now, and we could have a cuppa.'

I thought, Trust the British, turning to a cuppa in every emergency. Do I sound as stupid as I feel? Why can't I think of the right thing to say?

'Got to get back. Cousins. They'll worry. But I had to get out for a bit. Had to be by myself.'

He continued to look at me like a puppy begging for instructions, so I got hold of his arm again, and walked

29

him to his gate. He was in shock, and I didn't how to cope. It occurred to me I ought to say I was sorry, but I didn't know what words to use. It was really embarrassing.

'Hi!' Kate and Luke were on top of us before I saw them. Kate was hugging her school bag, and Luke was walking along on the outside of her. The perfect little gentleman.

Rocco turned round and looked at them. He seemed to know them, which was an improvement on his previous state. 'Hi,' he said.

'Something wrong?' said Luke, shouldering his bag.

Rocco's face sort of folded over on itself, and I looked away. It's not done to watch a boy cry.

'Hey, what's up?' Kate whispered to me.

'He's just heard his parents have been killed in a bombing attack.'

'How awful!' whispered Kate.

Luke had his arm round Rocco's shoulders, and was holding him tight. Rocco was making ghastly noises, sort of eeyore-ing. Horrid. Churned me up.

Kate started patting his shoulder, looking as if she'd rather be somewhere else, which was my feeling exactly.

Luke said to us, 'You two go on. I'll see you tomorrow at school. I'll go in with him for a bit.'

He went indoors with Rocco, and I started wheeling my bike along the pavement.

'That's awful!' said Kate, again.

I nodded. It really was. It put things into perspective a bit, too. I'd thought I'd got problems, had I? I didn't know I was born. Kate left me at our gate, and went on down to the flats where she lived.

Mum was in the kitchen when I got in. Before I met Rocco, I'd been rehearsing how I could break it to her about losing my place in the top set for English, but now it seemed unimportant, so I just sat down and ate my tea and let her rabbit on.

My mum is a big woman with curly brown hair, and eyes that pin down anything that moves. She's a whizz at accounting, and has a part-time job with a local firm, doing their books.

She does drone on a bit, though.

'. . . so I explained to my boss about Derek's being made redundant and asked if he could give me a couple of hours more each week, or even let me work full time, but he said they can't manage that at the moment, though if things improve, and interest rates come down, then . . .'

A good try, I thought. Pity it hadn't come off. How on earth was I going to tell her?

'. . . as it is, I think I can keep up with the mortgage repayments, and maybe we can manage a fortnight's holiday in the country with my sister. I rang the travel agency and cancelled our booking for Greece. Luckily we'd only paid the deposit, and they were sympathetic, so maybe we'll get even the deposit back . . .'

I pulled a face. I'd been looking forward to Greece.

'. . . and I was just thinking to myself, coming along, thank heavens you're doing all right at school. I feel so sorry for that woman down the road with the backward child. It's costing her the earth in extra tuition, and I doubt if the boy will ever get anywhere. Which reminds

31

me, haven't you got any homework?'

I felt myself go red, but she didn't notice. 'Mr Toft's away, and we had old Snowcem. He was foul. But we didn't get any English homework, and I did the rest in break. By the way, you know the boy we call 'Rocco', across the road? His parents have been killed in a bombing raid.'

'No! These ghastly bombings, when will they ever learn . . . ?'

I went upstairs, and fell back full length onto the bed. Rocco, Snowcem, Earl Grey. Aargh! I'd like to twist Snowcem's skinny neck right off his bony shoulders. I could scream, only Mum would come, wanting to know what was wrong.

I can't tell her. Not yet.

There must be some way to get round it.

I could go to see old Toft in the hospital. If I knew which hospital, which I don't . . .

The others will laugh. Kate will pretend to be upset for me but she'll smile about it behind my back and shrug, and say, Well, what did you expect?

I hate Kate, and Snowcem and if Earl Grey tries to . . . I'll . . . I'll . . .

My foot jarred the table, and one of my cardboard penguins fell over. I kicked the table quite deliberately, and another fell over and lay on top of the first.

I sat up and glared at them. I'd placed a whole row of cut-out penguins across the front of the model theatre I was making.

That's my hobby, by the way. I make model theatres. They're not toys. They're made of wood and some of them even have electric light circuits in them. I've got six of them on a shelf above my bed, but the one I was working on then was only half finished. I'd come unstuck over some elaborate scenery, and then I'd got bored with cutting out all the itsy bitsy little figures, and I'd got this picture of black and white adelie penguins, and I'd mounted it on a card, and cut them out.

I like penguins, always have. Mum says it's because I had a favourite stuffed penguin toy when I was tiny. I chewed its flippers off. I can remember the taste of the felt to this day. They bought me another one later, but it wasn't the same. It was an adelie penguin, all black and white. They're the smallest and the cutest in Antarctica.

But that day I didn't like penguins. I didn't like anything. I threw the model theatre on the floor, and jumped on it till it was mashed into pieces. I was crying. I don't know why. There wasn't anything to cry about, really. If I wasn't going to be an academic wonder, then that's the way it was going to have to be. I'd have to accept it, and get on with my life, and to hell with Snowcem and Toft and Earl Grey.

If they didn't think I was worth educating, then I'd show them what I could do in other ways. I'd make their lives hell. I knew I could.

It was a good feeling.

Mum came in and said, 'What on earth are you doing?'

I brushed my arm up over my face to clean it. 'Nothing much. It just wasn't working out properly. I'm fed up with theatres, anyway. I think I'll go out on my bike for a while.'

3

Dec 12 **VOLUNTEER BEACH** Arr 0700 Dep 1130

Weather: cloudy (clowdy?), SSW wind.

The ship's log says: a wild ride and wet landing at sandy Volunteer beach. The morning was spent with the king penguins that dominate the area. (The ride inshore on the Zodiac was hairy! King penguins are al right, much larger than the others. They seemed as curius (cureous?) about us as we were about them).

PORT STANLEY *Arr 1330 Dep 1700*

Weather: cloudy.

Ship's log: an afternoon visit to the port of Stanley, capital of the Falklands Islands. Guided tour to the museum and war memorials. Shopping for soovenirs. (This place is something else!)

Sam's alternative: It was a good day. I really enjoyed it. Seeing the signs marked 'Minefields' gave me a thrill. I did the usual joking act about it, but it does rather make for gooseflesh. Do you know, they call everything outside the immediate townships 'camp'. I bought some super stamps. I don't think I'd fancy living here for good, though.

The company on board improves on acquaintance. I never thought to see all those crocks hopping up and down ladders and in and out of boats as they do. Some of them get as far as the shore, look at the cliff they'd have to climb to get anywhere, and decide that's enough exercise for the day, thank you. So they get back into the Zodiacs – they're a kind of inflatable go-everywhere boat – and return to the ship. Not me. I want to do everything, see everything. I quite like the bloke in charge of one of the Zodiacs. He's straightforward. He could see I knew something about the penguins, and he showed me round a bit on land.

Thinking about penguins beforehand, I'd wondered if I'd be amazed when I saw them in person. If they'd look or act different from the way I'd been thinking of them. They don't. They're just more real. I can't explain it properly, but when I saw them on telly, or in the zoo, they looked a bit . . . freakish. The comics of creation. All that ungainly weight being shuffled around on flippers. Occasionally they'd slip and slither around and make a meal of the simplest action, like walking up a slope. Well, who wouldn't, if they were built like that? Typical sea-side postcard; elderly and portly gent slips on banana skin. But somehow they don't look comical, here.

They're more intelligent than I'd thought. They react to our two-footed invasion more like a crowd of people than a crowd of birds. We get too near them and they all move down to the water as if there was only one mind at work in all those bodies. Then we stop moving, and they stop and look back at us, and somehow you can feel what they're thinking . . . like, are we a threat, or a diversion?

They are as curious about us, as we are about them. They look at us, sort of sideways, with such a knowing, energetic look . . . and come to think of it, they're two-footed persons, themselves. They belong here, and we don't.

Enough of penguins.

I don't go in for boyfriends, like Kate does. I mean, I have friends who are boys, and usually they're easier to get along with than girls. Kate is not so much a friend as something I got stuck with the day we started playgroup together.

I was sorry when Kate made a set at Luke. He hadn't a chance, poor lad. All that strawberries and cream and goo-goo eyes. But she didn't get it all her own way, because Luke has a flaw . . . he's a sucker for a sob story, and there was Rocco, suffering all over the place. Not even Kate could distract Luke from Rocco. Not that she didn't try.

We were in the playground at break. Rocco had gone off to get us drinks from the machine outside the canteen. Kate and Luke were sitting on a bench, and I was doing press-ups on the ground beside them. If I couldn't shine at games, at least I could keep fit, and if Earl Grey said just once more that she thought I'd be happier in the remedial class, I'd pick her up by her teensy weensy little arms and chuck her through the nearest window.

Kate said, 'I know you want to be a doctor, Luke . . .'

It was the first I'd heard of it, but it made sense.

'. . . but you have to make time for yourself, give yourself some space. You can't go on nannying Rocco for ever. You hardly let him cross the road by himself.'

'It takes time. He'll come out of it, soon.'

'Did you have to give him your packed lunch?'

'He left his at home, and anyway, I only gave him half. My good deed for the day.' Luke made it sound comical, but I thought he probably meant it. Kate must have thought so, too, because she frowned, and Kate didn't believe in frowning, because of the horrid things it did to one's skin.

I said, 'You're not a scout or anything, are you?'

Luke saluted. 'My country, right or wrong!'

'Be serious,' said Kate. 'I mean, I was in the Brownies with Sam ages ago and then she was a Guide for a while, but we grew out of all that.'

'All what?' said Luke. 'Helping people?'

Kate couldn't exactly say 'yes,' but that was obviously what she meant.

'I'm a Christian,' said Luke. 'Is that what you mean?'

Kate blushed, and I stopped doing press-ups to see if he were serious. He was. Then I looked at Kate, to see how she was taking it. Luke was looking at Kate as if what she said next really mattered, but then, he looked at everyone like that. Kate didn't seem to know whether to smile or frown. As far as I knew, she hadn't been inside a church since she left Brownies.

'Yes,' said Luke, answering unspoken questions, 'I do go to church, usually. I was a member of the youth club at our church where we lived before, and I'm hoping to find a friendly place to go to now. And yes, it does mean a lot to me.'

Kate said, 'Oh, I didn't mean to . . . well . . . I don't go now, but I used to. Sam's people go, now and then.'

Luke turned his shining gaze on me. 'Where do you go? What's it like? Is there a good youth group?'

It was my turn to feel embarrassed. 'The parents go to the church on the Green. I go with them sometimes. The youth club's a bit young. There is something on a Sunday evening for our age group, but it sounds boring and there's homework to do, so I don't go.'

'Yes, there's always homework,' said Luke, and I

couldn't make out if he were laughing at me or not.

I tried to change the subject. 'I vote we get Rocco along to the Drama Club.'

'Mm,' said Kate, looking pleased. 'And you, Luke. They always need boys. I'm trying out for the juvenile lead in the next play. It's "South Pacific". Sam will be working backstage so we'll all be together.'

'OK,' said Luke. 'You're on.'

Nothing more was said about Luke spending so much time with Rocco, and they did both join the Drama Club. Rocco still acted little boy lost, but most of us could cope with that in small doses. I suppose Kate did get her own way really, because she got to see more and not less of Luke. She was sorry for Rocco, too, but like me, she didn't know what to say to him.

It wasn't as if Luke were the only one who rallied around. Lots of people did. I mean, I used to take videos round there and watch them with him when he was baby-sitting for his little cousins – and a couple of little terrors they were, too, I can tell you. A lad from Rocco's football team went round there, too. We tried to get Rocco back onto the football field, but he'd lost his zing, if you see what I mean. Hardly stirred out of the house. Wouldn't even have gone to school if one of us hadn't called for him every day.

I reckon, looking back, that's what kept me at school, even in Earl Grey's class. If there is a teacher anywhere on this earth worse than Earl Grey, don't tell me about her, because I don't want to know. Why the nickname 'Earl' Grey? Because she was weak, and Earl Grey tea is weak. OK?

I played her up, but my heart wasn't really in it. I reckon if I'd really tried, I could have got myself expelled, and the parents would have found out even sooner than they did.

And guess what! Old Snowcem wasn't content with bunging me out of his class. He had to go and tell every other member of the staff what he'd done, hadn't he? I soon found out I had ceased to be flavour of the month with the maths and biology teachers. That was when I decided there was no point in even trying to do my homework, so I got put on report. That meant I had to take my work for assessment every week to one of the Deputy Heads. That was a laugh. I turned up, she said 'Tut, tut, you must try to do better!' and I went away again.

I was within that much of dropping out of school altogether. In fact, I was thinking of trying to get a Saturday job in the delicatessen down the road, for a start. I thought I could tell the parents I was trying to help out now that Dad was unemployed. And then I could sort of slide out of school and into work and they'd hardly notice, except for being glad I was bringing a little money into the house instead of taking it out all the time.

I reckon I would have done, too, if the sky hadn't fallen on me first. The 'sky' in this case being Parents' Evening.

To tell the truth, I'd put it out of my mind. If I'd thought about it maybe I'd have prepared the parents for what they were going to hear, but I'd sort of thought it might be easier to tell them if I'd got a proper job lined up first. I'd tried the deli and they said OK, but wouldn't give me more than Saturday afternoon till I was sixteen, and that wasn't going to be for another couple of months. I'd started working there, cutting and slicing and packing and giving change – and I had to be slow and careful over that, I can tell you. Anyway, I thought that once I'd been there for a while, they'd look more kindly on my full-time application, and Parents' Evening sort of crept up on me without my noticing.

And there was the show we were doing, as well. That stupid idiot of a Stage Manager got himself re-appointed for 'South Pacific', and my only consolation was that I was made his official sidekick. Which meant, in practice, that I had to take over on the nights when he couldn't make it.

Back home, I built myself a scale replica of the school stage, knocked up some scenery and lights, and went through all the changes and cues. After a while I began to think how it might be done with a better lighting rig, and better sets. I actually designed and made some new scenery, and got a lot of fun playing around with it.

It gave me a shock, sometimes, in the middle of a rehearsal, to remember how limited were the resources I actually had to play with, backstage at school.

I used the money from the deli job to go up Town and get gallery seats in theatres, trying to work out how many lights they had, and how they did the sound effects and changed the scenery. There's a chap up in the West End, they say he can follow a bouncing tennis ball with his 'spot'. That's 'spotlight' to you. There's people spend all their professional lives just operating spotlights. I wonder if I could learn how . . . but not in the school theatre, that's for sure.

Mrs Whittle, the Drama teacher, used to hate me. That was because when we did drama in our second year at High School, she made us dance around and pretend to be robots and people dying of grief, and all that guff. Kate can do all that sort of thing on her head, but I was hopeless at it. So I used to clown about to cover up, and then she'd screech at me.

So when I first turned up in the Drama Club, she set her teeth and was obviously working out how to get rid of me, until I said I wanted to learn backstage work. After that she came round to the idea that I wasn't bad at it, and when that stupid clot of a 4th year was discovered smoking in the cupboard where they keep the paints and solvents, she didn't hesitate too long before offering me the job.

I didn't rat on him, let me tell you. Kate found him there and screeched her head off, being the sort that's pretty quick to see danger if it affects her. I suppose she was right, too. I mean, everyone knew he was bunking off to smoke in stupid places, but it's one thing knowing, and another thing actually blowing the gaff. Did Kate know what she was going to find when she opened the door? I don't know. Best not ask. Sometimes it's hard to know whether she does things consciously or otherwise.

It was about this time that Kate and Luke had their big fall out. She'd got him accompanying her everywhere by being sympathetic about Rocco, and so they got into the habit of walking back home together, the three of them. And going to football matches together. Not that

Luke played, but Rocco went back to it, after a while. They even joined me in cheering now and then. Rocco's not a bad full back, when he puts his mind to it, but even Kate could see that he needed to put on a bit of weight to get back into top form. I used to sneak him bits of extra from the deli, and when Kate got to find out, she made him some fudge and gave everyone else a piece, too. She does that sort of thing so gracefully, everyone admired her both for her cooking and her charity!

Then Luke started on at us about going to church on Sunday evenings. He'd been to the church on the Green that the parents go to, and he'd found out there was this evening meeting, and he sort of assumed – I honestly think he's not too bright sometimes – that Kate and Rocco and I would go along with him.

I could see Kate wondering how to get out of it, and Rocco looking at Luke all dog-like and devoted and obviously willing to do anything if it kept him in with Luke.

I said, 'Sorry, I have a previous engagement.' Which I had, with the telly. There was a new murder mystery starting that Sunday evening, and I wouldn't have missed it for the world. I'm potty about murder mysteries, but they've got to be well done, mind! None of that 'let's walk through the routine, we all know how this sort of thing goes' type of thing.

Kate did her 'I'm not going to frown' act, and said she'd been asked out by a lower sixth year bloke, which I thought was a lie, but turned out to be nothing but the truth. Actually, he was playing opposite her in 'South

Pacific', and I suppose he thought she was up to what he wanted in a girl, and maybe she was.

Luke looked at me, and I thought, He's disappointed. I was sorry about that, but not sorry enough to miss my programme.

We might have known getting the juvenile lead in 'South Pacific' would go to Kate's head. Suddenly she didn't want to hang around with us so much. She even walked home with her sixth former, instead of us. Now that's just not on. You stick with your friends in your own age group or you lose them, and no-one except Luke had a good word to say for her when she started on that lark. She stopped working – not that she'd ever done much in that line – and announced she was going to send her photos to 'The Clothes Show', as she intended to be a model when she left school.

Now her sixth former, Ben, was into photography, and soon she was showing us the photos he'd taken of her. They weren't bad, but they were a bit, I don't know, corny. A bit sixties starlet, if you know what I mean. I didn't think they did her justice, because she could look all right at times, when she wasn't trying too hard. She even got told off at school about that time for shoving so much make-up on her face. I reckon that must be the first time in her life she ever got told off at school. It was disgusting, honest, to see the way she spread it on her face, with a knife, almost.

So one night at rehearsal, I rigged up this bucket of water, with a rope from the girder over the stage, and a nylon cord leading to where I could operate it from by the curtains. I was all set to deluge her when she was singing her duet with her lovey-dovey sixth former, Ben. How I kept a straight face, I don't know. I'd been working it out for ages, and thinking about it on and off all that day.

The only thing I regretted was that I hadn't got a camera to immortalise the moment when the heavens opened on her. But neither of the parents would let me borrow theirs, and I'd never bothered with such things before, and of course there wasn't enough money coming into the house to ask for one for myself.

What would have been interesting, would have been to get her snapped by her beloved sixth former with his own camera, but I couldn't work out how to organise that. I mean, there he was on stage with her, and he didn't bring his camera to rehearsal.

So there they were, holding hands and looking into one another's eyes . . . my hand reached out for the cord and . . .

And Luke came up behind me, and caught hold of my wrist.

4

He said in a fierce whisper, 'Sam, what on earth . . . !'

As if he couldn't see what I intended to do!

I tried to wrench my wrist away, but he hung on. He's stronger than he looks.

'Let go of me!' I whispered back.

He wouldn't. He hadn't done any shouting, but all that pulling and pushing had caught Kate's eye. She stopped singing, and gaped at us. Her beloved also stopped singing, and twisted round to see what was happening. They looked at the cord in my hand, and followed it up to where the pail of water was rocking above them.

'Ouch!' cried Kate, as a couple of drops hit her.

'Look out!' Her beloved gave her a push and sent her sprawling. Chivalry incarnate.

I said a bad word, and Luke wrested the cord from my hand. I fell headlong onto the stage, which brought

Mrs Whittle up, demanding to know what was the matter.

'Nothing,' said Luke, tossing the free end of the cord up onto a stage flat nearby. 'Sam had a spider on her shoulder, and I was trying to get it off.'

Beloved sixth former looked as if he were going to spill the beans, but Kate was too quick for him. 'Yes, and he flicked it on me, and I screamed. I hate spiders!'

Mrs Whittle blinked at Kate and then at me. I was on my feet again, and feeling murderous.

'Let's take it again then, shall we?' said Mrs Whittle. The piano started pounding out the notes again, and Kate and her sixth former tried to recapture Love's first careless rapture, but it wasn't a very good try. They were too conscious of the pail of water balanced overhead. So was Luke. He stood there arms akimbo, grimly waiting till the rehearsal broke up. Then he watched while I got a ladder, brought the pail down, and threw the water away.

I was too mad to speak to him, and I certainly wasn't going to apologise.

He didn't wait for Kate, or for me, but went off with Rocco. I sulked behind the flats till I thought Kate had gone, and then fell over her, crying in a corner.

Now Kate doesn't cry, period.

I suppose I gaped at her. She huddled away from me, sniffing.

Kate does not sniff. I mean, it's such an ungraceful, unromantic, ordinary thing to do.

I can sniff. You can sniff. Kate does not sniff.

I couldn't have been more astonished if she'd stood on

her head, which, as you can imagine, no-one has ever seen Kate do.

I took a quick look around, but everyone had gone. They'd even turned off the lights, backstage.

I suppose she thought she was alone.

I crept back a pace or two, and thought about just sneaking away. She'd hate to have anyone see her like that. I mean, not her usual self at all. Quite frankly, she looked awful.

I told myself she hadn't wanted anyone to see her cry, and that included me. Then I thought maybe I could take the opportunity to say I was sorry for the trick I'd nearly played on her, and then I could go with a clear conscience.

I hate apologising. It makes my blood pressure rise to have to apologise for anything. I could feel my neck going red as I tried to work myself up to apologising.

I got it out, somehow. 'Er, sorry, Kate, for . . . you know . . . er . . . got a hankie?'

She smothered some words in her hands, put her head between her knees and howled.

Oh, golly whatsits. What was I supposed to do?

Leave her?

It would be best, surely. Let her recover by herself.

Luke wouldn't have left her like that, I suppose. But thinking about what Luke would do, gave me an uneasy feeling that he was at the bottom of this thunderstorm.

Bother him. Why did he have to come along and upset us like this? If it hadn't been for him . . .

Stop. You're being stupid.

Do something, girl. Don't just stand there. Do something.

I went and got a handful of paper towels from the loo, and pushed them into her hands. She kept her hands over her face, though, so I helped her to her feet, steered her into the loo, ran the water and got her to wash. She kept making funny little gasping sounds all the time. You couldn't call them words. Distress signals, I suppose you could call them.

'So what's all this about?' I asked, when she had got as far as wondering – in a whisper – where she'd left her school bag with her comb in it.

She burst out crying again.

Honestly!

I'd got some chocolate in my bag, so I fed it to her because it was supposed to buck you up when you were down. She ate it with her eyes on the ground, and then started to fuss about her hair.

She gave me a fleeting, squinting glance over her arm as she combed her hair. This was not the Kate we all knew and tolerated. This was one very mixed-up kid.

I said, 'So what's wrong? Apart from me, I mean.'

She sighed from her toes upwards. 'Nothing.'

'Come on, you can tell me.'

'Oh, Samantha, I'm so miserable!'

'I can see that, idiot! You can't be this upset just because I was going to wash some of the makeup off your face!'

She showed signs of breaking forth in tears again, so I said that if she did, I'd slosh her one. That held back the floodgates for a bit.

She gulped once or twice, and said, 'I know it was

silly, but I thought I could make Luke jealous, and then . . . then . . . honest, I couldn't care less about Ben, he's a right berk. But it didn't work, did it? You saw. Luke just walked away. And oh, Samantha, I really do love him, you know.'

'What? Who? Luke?'

She gave a little wail, and hid her face in her hands. 'Don't laugh at me! I can't help it!'

'I'm not laughing.' And I wasn't. I was dead sorry for her, because honest, she'd jogged me into realising something very odd about Luke. He's cold inside, that's what it is. I don't know why it hadn't occurred to me before, but I suppose it's because he's all warm and caring on the outside, like with Rocco and anyone in trouble. But inside there was something, I don't know, not exactly 'cold' perhaps, but 'detached'. Yes, that was a better word. Detached. I could see that if Kate had come up against that, she'd feel it.

I sat there on the concrete floor, thinking about it.

She sniffed once or twice and said, 'We were getting on fine, seeing each other home from school and in the Drama Club, and we went to the Barn Dance at the church a couple of weeks ago, and then he said would I go with him and Rocco to this meeting on Sunday night, and I went, and they were all sitting around being so . . . so smug! Honestly, Samantha, it was unbearable!

'I tried to pretend that I knew what they were talking about, but I didn't, and I could feel Luke looking at me, and he must have thought I was totally clueless. And there was this other girl who obviously fancied him, you can tell, can't you, and she started making remarks about beginners, and I knew she meant me, and Luke gave me such a look, and I thought I was really showing him up before his friends . . .'

'Come on, now! Luke's not that sort.'

'. . . oh, he shut her up at the time, but I could see what he was thinking, that he was wishing he hadn't taken me. And they started talking about things I didn't understand, and that girl, she did it on purpose, I could see that, even if he couldn't . . . and Luke tried to get me into the discussion, but I knew if I said anything at all, I'd show him up, so I said I'd got a headache and wanted to go home, and Luke came away with me, but you could see he really wanted to stay, so I got cross with him, which was stupid . . .'

She paused for a gulp, and I thrust another paper towel in her hands for a quick blow and wipe up.

'. . . and I started picking on him on the way home, and he just got more and more patient with me, but I could see he was not pleased underneath, and I felt so awful, and I said he needn't bother to wait for me after school because someone else wanted to walk home with me and . . . and he thought I meant it!'

I wanted to say, 'Is he worth it?' But I suppose to her he was.

She said, 'I told Mum about it, and she said I should play hard to get, and he'd soon realise what he was missing, but it hasn't worked, has it, and I'm sure he thinks I'm just a silly flirt, without a serious thought in my head . . .'

Which was my own view, exactly. I could hardly say so, though.

'Mm,' I said, encouragingly.

She turned to me, then. 'Do you think I should apologise to Luke? I mean, I could send him a note, and ask to talk to him, to get things straightened out, and then . . . and then . . .'

'. . . and then he'd ask you to go back to the church group with him, and what would you do then?'

'I don't know.'

She got to her feet and dusted herself down.

'You're right, of course,' she said. 'He's just not my type. I just . . . went overboard or something. I wish I'd never asked him to join the Drama Club. I never want to see him again.'

A fat lot of use that line of talk was going to be, since we were all in the same school together. Anyway, I got her collected together and walked my bike home with her. I don't know why other people don't go to school by bike. Or I do, rather. Kate would look pretty daft in her short skirt, riding a bike. Culottes? Don't make me laugh. She thinks they're 'deeply unfeminine'.

She didn't talk much on the way home. I didn't feel like talking, either. I was sorry for her, the silly cow.

Also, I was trying to remember something someone had told me once about people who went to church. Something about them not wanting to get tied up with people who didn't believe in God. Maybe that was what had got into Luke. Or maybe he'd just been pushed a bit too far too quickly by Kate, or by the girl who ran the youth group.

Kate was a lot prettier than most girls. I thought she could give anyone a run for their money in that line. If

I'd been her, I'd have gone back to the group, and stuck it out. Learned about whatever it was they were on about, and kept close to Luke that way. But Kate didn't seem to cope with criticism all that well. Perhaps because she so rarely came across it.

When we got to her flats, she said, 'Well, thanks,' and hung around looking at me as if waiting for me to say something.

I said, 'You don't think it would be a good idea to go back to the group and find out what it's all about? Show him you're serious about it?'

She shook her head. 'They'd only say I was chasing him. I'll get over it. I'll have to. There's no future in it. But thanks, Samantha. I really appreciate . . . everything.'

She dodged towards me, and for an awful moment I thought she was going to try to kiss me, and so I pulled back. She laughed a bit and looked embarrassed. Then she touched me on the arm, and went off into the flats.

I was sorry for her but I also wondered, cynically, how long it would be before she'd be going out with someone else. Our Katie's not that deep. Sweet and pretty, of course. But shallow.

Luke was well out of it.

The weather's awful here on ship. The winds are against us and they say we're in for worse, and won't be able to stop at Elephant Island. I don't think I care. I had another nightmare last night, and even woke my cabin mate up. I don't want to talk about it. I'm going up on Obs Deck.

If I spot the first iceberg, I get the champagne. That might cheer me up. And I suppose I might as well go to the lectures . . . some of them, anyway. I'll go to the Penguin one.

Dec 13 at sea on route to **ANTARCTICA**

Weather Overcast, SSW winds

Ship's log: Gutsy 35–40 kt winds swayed the ship as we entered the dreaded Drake Passage. Lots of birdwatching. There were three lectures. I enjoyed the one on 'Penguins: their history, behaviour and ecology.' That was OK. Then there was one on Glaciology, which I thought would have been interesting but wasn't. I went to the one on 'The Antarctic Treaty and Geopolitics' because it was all about the different nations having bases down here and what each base does. I never knew there were so many bases down here. I wonder if it ever gets like the Tower of Babel, with so many nationalities.

Dec 14 at sea en route to **ANTARCTICA**

Weather: overcast, SSW winds

Steaming towards the South Shetlands Islands. Lots of

lectures. I qwote: 'Who were the Heroes?' a discussion
of Antarctic exploration.' Lecture: Biographical sketch
of Sir Ernest Shackleton, and viewing of original
footage from the Endurance Expedition. Lecture:
'Antarctic Seals.' Late night video of Jack Hanna's
Voyage to Antarctica, on the World Discoverer.

I can't be bothered with my own log today.

Dec 15 BRANSFIELD STRAIT (cruising)

Weather: Overcast/snow, SSW winds

Ship's log: the wind picked up to gusty 50 kts and foiled
our attempt to visit Elephant Island. Instead, we steamed
towards Deception Island thru' the Bransfield Strait.
(Notes: 1st iceberg spotted, approx 4.15 am, also 2
ships, probly trawlers on the edge of sight in the mist.
I thought I saw the iceberg first, but someone else got
the prize. Typical.)
Lecture: 'Current Antarctic Seabird Research.'

I hate everything!

5

Dec 16 **BAILEY HEAD, DECEPTION ISL.**
Arr 0530 Dep 0830

Weather overcast, var winds

*Ship's log: landed at Bailey's beach, saw thousands of
chinstrap penguins. Uphill hike to the rookery.*
  *(Note: Volcano – last eruption 1970 destroyed the
settlement at Whalers Bay. Seen at Bailey Head:
chinstrap penguins, adelie penguin who'd got lost.
Chinstraps were sitting on eggs, the nests are made of
pebles in order to keep the egg above water melt level.)*

WHALERS BAY, DECEPTION ISL. *Arr 0900*
Dep 1230

*Ship's log: threaded our way through Neptune's
Bellows, the narrow entrance to the caldera of
Deception Island. Anchored opposite the ruins of the
British Antarctic Survey Station. Eerie place.
Explored the colony of the Antarctic terns and pintado
petrels.*

*(Notes: Marty, one of Zodiac drivers, & I then
walked along the ridge – firm snow all the way up
from the beach. Hiked across to Neptune's window. Saw
where hot springs come up through sea; stink of
sulphur, lots of steam off water. Realy odd).*

HANNAH PT., LIVINGSTON ISL. *Arr 1330*
Dep 1900

*In the afternoon, saw gentoo, chinstrap and macaroni
penguins with their day old chicks. Also a number of
Weddell seal, elephant seal and hundreds of blue-eyed
shags. Gleaming Antarctic sunset as we cruised further
south towards the Gerlache Strait.*

*(Notes: Hannah Point named after a whaling ship.
Blue eyed shags are the only Antarctic bird who hatch
naked & blind 2–4 in a clutch. Macaronis are v rare in
Antarctic penninsula. Same family as Rockhoppers*

58

with orange crests above the eyes. Some gulls deserted their nests when we came ashore. Therefore, the expedition leaders have decided not to bring visitors to Hannah Point at this time of year again.)

This was the best yet! A whole day with the penguins, and I think I've got them all sorted out now. The chinstraps are easy, because they've got a black mark like a strap under their chins. The rockhoppers have got little tufts on their heads. The adelies are the smallest, perhaps the most graceful – if you can call penguins graceful.

Yes, you can call them graceful. When they're in the water they're magic. And you can't really complain about the way they're built, because they're purpose built and adapted for life where they are. I'll never call a penguin clumsy again.

It gives me a really warm feeling to watch them. The seals, most of them, are horrible. They give me the shivers. So large and . . . well, enormous. I can't cope with large things. They make me feel threatened, even though we don't go that near them. We saw one eat a penguin. Pure horror movie, and don't say it's only nature, because I know it is, but . . .

I had a long talk with Marty. He's nice, very straightforward. He trained as a biologist but got bored with the course and was going to drop out. His family went frantic, wanting him to have a nice white collar job, safe pension and all that. But he got offered a job as a Zodiac driver, so after he got his degree, he upped and came down here and has been living on the boat ever since, doing just what comes naturally. I think that's pretty brave of him. Of course, he has still got his degree, so if he wants to go back and do something 'normal' later on, he can. We talked a bit about what I plan to do. Nice of him to bother. I wish I could be more like him.

I'm feeling rotten. Three nights of nightmares. It's amazing I'm still on my feet. It was weird, the storm coming, and the ship having to fight its way through the heavy seas against the wind. I spent a lot of time on the Obs deck, but you couldn't take both hands off the rail to take photos, because you'd have been blown away if you had. The lectures were all right, I suppose. The others really enjoyed them, and they passed the time. But I can't take that many lectures at once. The penguin one was good, of course.

I spent a lot of time trying not to think. I don't know why I started this looking-back lark. It's sent me into a real 'downer' of a mood. I'd forgotten a lot of what happened, except in general terms.

When I played back what I'd recorded, I wanted to erase it, and say that wasn't how it happened, and of course I didn't join the group just to spite Kate. But that's what I did. I wanted to show them, especially Kate, that I could do something she couldn't do.

I am not a nice person.

I try to pretend that I don't care what people think about me, but of course I do.

I joined the Sunday night group for all the wrong reasons, and I wasn't straight with them, either, about why I joined. I said my parents had been pushing me to join. Well, of course, they thought it was a good idea, but they'd given up trying to make me go to church, so although it sounded all right, it wasn't the truth. The group accepted my reason, though, and Luke and Rocco gave me such a welcome as never was, making room for me to sit between them, and explaining things to me as we went along.

I'd joined at an odd time, you see, because they weren't just having their ordinary meetings but actually preparing to take part in an evening service. They did that once a year, choosing all the hymns and choruses, and playing guitars and tambourines and using the overhead projector and acting out sketches.

I wondered how on earth Kate had managed to miss an opportunity to shine on stage, but I soon realised the group already had its own 'star'. Maybe Kate hadn't been keen on sharing the limelight. Or maybe she hadn't understood enough of what was going on.

I'm not sure that I took it in at first, either. It was a sketch about Jesus asking Peter to follow him without asking questions, without returning home first to pack, or to wait for his friends. It left a sourish taste in the mouth, I don't know why. It just did.

The leader wasn't the girl whom Kate had been complaining about, but a boy who was going on to do acting somewhere. He was a brilliant mime, I'll give him that. They got Luke to act the part of Jesus, and this other boy, the mimic, he took Peter.

I was told to help out with the chorus bits, but I asked if I could do ASM, and they said OK, so I held things and passed things and generally took part without having to stick my neck out. Then we had a discussion about us all saying a form of the creed. You know, what we believed about God, and Jesus and the resurrection and all that. They said there'd been lots of versions, and we were going to make up our own, that we didn't all have to believe all of it all the time, but have a majority viewpoint on it.

That wasn't bad, because on the whole I'd rather believe than not, and I knew what they were talking about from having been to church with my parents when I was a child. Most of the time I do believe there is a God, and I believe in Jesus, too. I wasn't so sure about the resurrection bit, but some of the others weren't sure either, so the argument was quite amiable.

I wouldn't say I was committed to the group, but I had lots of time on my hands then, because of dropping homework. The parents were redecorating the house from top to bottom while Dad was still looking for jobs, and Mum was fairly uptight, what with keeping her own job going, and worrying about the mortgage.

No-one paid much attention to me at home, and that was fine by me. Kate took to walking to and from school with another girl from our class, and I got Rocco to get himself some wheels, and we used to catch up with Luke at the corner and go on together.

The play at school came off better than we could have hoped, though Kate didn't sparkle quite as much as she'd been expected to do. Ben, her sixth former, had got himself another good-looker to hang about with. I took over as Stage Manager. That was OK, too.

It was all, you might say, satisfactory.

Except that I came face to face with Kate one day, and realised that everything we'd ever had in common had disappeared. We were both at the same school still, of course, but there wasn't a single class we now had together. I think she was going to say something, but I cut her off with the excuse that I was waiting for Mrs Whittle. Kate went on, hugging her school-bag to herself as she usually does. That girl will have a stoop before long, if she'd not careful.

The Whittle wanted to know if I were available in the school holidays to go on some course or other that she was taking. If it had been just drama, I'd have said 'No', but it was backstage work as well, in a proper theatre with professional if slightly out of date equipment. The family weren't going to be away for more than a few days, so I said I would, and she said, 'See you next term!' meaning I could do the SM's job in the winter production.

That gave me a jolt, because I'd planned to leave school at the end of term, when I would be close to my sixteenth birthday. But she'd gone before I could explain. I shrugged. Sufficient to the day is the evil thereof. I know where *that* comes from. The Bible. It's odd how things that Gran used to say to me come back at different times.

Every birthday she used to bring out the same story. She had a day by day tear off calendar, and on the day I was born, the Bible quote was something from Thessalonians about working with your hands. She said it was a sign to tell me what I should do with my life. Weird.

Anyway, when I'd said Hail and Farewell to Whittle,

I got my bike out and went home only to discover the parents fussing around, preparing for Open Evening at school. I'd forgotten all about it, to be truthful. Or not wanted to think about it, maybe.

I sat there eating sausages and baked beans, and wondering what I was going to do about it. I'd got them half way happy about my Saturday job in the deli, but hadn't actually got as far as breaking the news to them that I was leaving school that summer. You can smooth things like that over in your mind if you try, and I suppose I had tried. What was the point of agonising over something you couldn't do anything about? That was my line, and I had stuck to it.

Only, they didn't seem to have cottoned on at all. They were saying things like, 'We've been really looking forward to Parents' Evening . . . such a change to have something nice to look forward to . . .'

I considered going sick. I could get the thermometer and dip it in my hot tea and pretend I'd got a fever. I could say I had a bug. There's always a bug of some sort going around.

Then I thought I might as well go through with it. If the parents heard for themselves exactly how small were my hopes of getting any GCSEs, then perhaps there would be one short sharp thunderstorm and I'd be free to go my own way.

So I changed into a sweatshirt and jogging trousers and went meekly off with them to school. It occurred to me, going along, that I ought to warn them so that it wouldn't give them heart attacks when they heard how bad everything was. But they wouldn't listen. They just sort of smiled and said, 'Yes, dear, I'm sure you've no need to be nervous . . . we quite understand . . .'

Only, of course, they didn't understand at all.

I guided them to Earl Grey's table, and stood beside them while she wittered on about how I was such a 'dear girl' and 'so full of character' and if only I could concentrate, she (Earl Grey) was sure that one of these fine days I'd find English wasn't so very difficult after all.

The parents blinked a bit at that, and asked how Mr Toft was getting on – I had told them Mr Toft was ill and I was in someone else's class, but it obviously hadn't meant anything to them.

'I'm afraid her exam results were not exactly shining . . .' said Earl Grey, looking tortured as she always does when brought face to face with her own inadequacies.

My father's eyes nearly bulged out of their sockets as he took in the result of the tests, and spotted – at last! – the fact that Earl Grey was not taking the First Set.

'What's this?' he said.

'I don't understand!' complained my mother. 'Samantha's always been in the top set for English.'

Earl Grey looked angrily at me. I suppose it would have been easier for her if I hadn't been there. I grinned back at her. It was up to her to explain to the parents. I'd tried, and hadn't got through.

She said, 'I'm afraid your daughter's attitude . . . I mean, that her general level of attainment . . . is not up to the standards of the First Set in English. In fact, I am surprised that she should ever have been considered for it.'

'You mean,' said my father, 'that she's been dropped from the First Set for English? But won't that affect her GCSEs?'

'I don't feel that we are very hopeful about Samantha obtaining high grades in . . .'

I stopped listening. Kate and her parents were queueing up at old Snowcem's table, while Luke and his mother were being talked at by the Old Boy himself. I gather Luke's father had gone off somewhere some time back, but that they were doing OK because Mrs had a good job, managing the fashion floor of a big department store. She was well turned out but never flashy, if you know what I mean.

Rocco was in the queue for the Biology table. He'd be all right even if he had taken a bit of a stumble last term. His uncle was with him.

'Well!' said my dad, pulling me and Mum away from Earl Grey. 'What have you to say to that, my girl?'

I shrugged. 'High School sorts out the men from the boys. I'd better leave at the end of the term, and get a job.'

'I don't understand!' said my mum. 'You've always been in the top sets right through school . . .'

'Well, I'm not, now.'

'Maths?' said my dad. I shook my head. 'Sciences . . . French . . . nothing?' He sounded shocked.

'I don't understand,' repeated my mum. 'How can she drop out like this?'

My dad looked around the crowded hall. 'Let's have

this out with your tutor for the year. Who is he?'

'It was Mr Toft, but he's still off sick. I've been going to one of the deputy heads for her to look at my work, but . . .'

'Which one?' He dragged me over to Miss Livingstone, and she, poor dear, looked sorry for my parents and even sorrier for herself because my dad got really angry during her report on my behaviour.

'. . . and you must see that it is extremely difficult for us to know how to deal with this when Samantha seems to be unable to help herself . . . homework not done . . . sloppy, careless work . . . ill-conceived practical jokes which amuse no-one . . . general don't care attitude . . .'

I shifted about a bit. Mum looked sick.

Dad looked as if he were going to throttle someone. Possibly me. Mum got out her handkerchief and blew her nose.

I was sorry for them. I wished things could have been different, that they'd had a clever daughter who'd done them credit. But I was I, and the sooner I was out of school the better.

We stood in a huddle outside the school gates. Dad was breathing hard, Mum wiping her eyes and blowing her nose.

I said, rather too loudly, 'I'm sorry. I didn't want to worry you, but they're right, and there's no point in my staying on at school. I can leave and get a job, and that'll help with the finances, won't it?'

'Not before you take your exams!' said my dad, but his heart wasn't in it.

'I don't understand!' whispered my mum, for the

umpteenth time. I wanted to put my arm around her and pet her, but we don't do that sort of thing in our family.

So I kicked an empty Coke tin around. There are always empty Coke tins hanging around our school gates, in spite of the bin the Council has put there.

Dad said, 'They ought to have warned us, earlier! If I'd known you were misbehaving, my girl . . .'

'It's all that Mr Toft's fault!' said Mum. 'If he hadn't gone sick . . . ! He always knew how to handle her!'

'. . . and after all our hopes for you!'

Well, the storm raged on. I put up my umbrella, and let it wash over me. I didn't enjoy it, of course. Who could enjoy putting an end to their parents' fond hopes for their offspring? Especially their one and only chick.

But I endured and managed not to say anything except that I was sorry, and that I had tried, really (which was not strictly true, but true enough). They went on at me all evening, with Mum dissolving into tears every now and then, and Dad glooming his way out into the garden and back again to deliver yet another diatribe against me.

I thought it would all be over more quickly if I let them get on with it, and I didn't even point out that they were missing one of their favourite telly programmes. Best to get it over with.

I could feel their disappointment heavy on my shoulders.

I wished . . . ah well. One had to put up with the kind of person one was.

The next day I didn't go to school, but cleaned the

kitchen stove while Dad went down the job centre yet again, and Mum bustled out to the morning's work. In the afternoon I helped them by painting the ceiling in the back bedroom. I kept thinking it was a weekend, but if it had been then I'd have been working at the deli. I wanted to go there and ask for a full-time job yet again, but Dad kept saying he didn't want me ending up in a dead end job. I reckoned any job was better than sitting about at home, sending out job applications and waiting for interviews that never materialised.

They'd come round to my way of seeing things soon enough.

At half past four, the doorbell rang and it was Luke, with Rocco hanging around at the gate. It was nice to see them. Luke came in, but Rocco waved and went on home.

I took Luke into the kitchen for a cuppa. He'd been in our house before, of course, watching videos, listening to tapes, that sort of thing. But this was different. He looked self-conscious for once. He usually gives the impression of being totally in command of whatever situation he's in.

He stirred sugar into his black coffee, and I knew he was upset, because he doesn't usually take sugar. I thought of pointing out what he'd done, and decided not to bother. He'd find out soon enough.

'The thing is,' he said, 'that I know I ought to have done something about this sooner. It's my fault it's gone on so long.'

'What has?'

'Your problem, disability, whatever you call it.'

'I'm not disabled.'

He went red. I'd never seen him embarrassed before. There was a sort of comfort in seeing him put out of countenance.

'Look,' he said, 'you don't have to drop out, as you have been doing. You don't have to accept Mr Snow's verdict . . . at least, what I mean is, you can do something about it. Or your parents can, rather. Do you want me to talk to them?'

'About what? Whatever for? I'm quite happy, thank you.'

'You can't be. Listen, we've all been praying about this . . .'

'Who has? What right have you to . . . !'

'. . . the right of a friend. You are part of us, and we are part of you, and naturally the group is worried about . . .'

'What group? The Sunday night lot?' I almost laughed in his face. Of course, he didn't know I'd only been going to the group to annoy Kate, and keep in with Luke himself. It had been an OK way of spending some of the time at weekends, but honest, that's all it had been. I saw he wouldn't understand, though, so I kept quiet.

'Of course the Sunday night group. Of course we've been praying for you, and talking about . . .'

'Talking about me behind my back? Thanks a bunch!'

'Well, we really do care what happens to you, and we've found out that you can get yourself assessed by a doctor outside the school, and he can give you a letter to get you extra time in exams, and that.'

'I'm not a dum-dum, thank you.'

'No, you're not. But you've let the school put you into that category, and if you aren't careful, it could ruin your life.'

'I know what I'm doing. I'm leaving school, in fact I've already left, and I'm going to get on with life as it really is, and not have to bother any more with stupid exams and homework.'

'You're too bright to . . .'

'No. Period. End of story.'

6

Luke took a mouthful of coffee, and practically threw up. Then he had a coughing fit, so I pounded him on the back, removed the sugared coffee, and got him some more. Unsugared.

He wiped his eyes and blew his nose. 'I'm handling this badly. I've thought about it so much, about what I should say. Now it's all gone. I know part of this is my fault. I ought to have talked it over with you before.'

'So why didn't you? Not that it would have made any difference. My mind was made up to leave ages ago, when Snowcem threw me out of the top set.'

'Well, first I didn't understand what was happening to you. I was new at the school and had to find my own way around. Then there was Rocco, and having to find a new church . . .'

'Excuses, excuses!'

'I know. I just didn't think. I'm sorry.' He fiddled around with his coffee. 'I suppose it's just another excuse, but you know things weren't easy at home, either.'

He hadn't ever talked about his mum before, or his dad leaving. I was human enough to be interested.

He sipped coffee. 'Dad going off like that . . . well, it kind of threw us both. Not that we'd ever been that close, as a family. I never remember him making time to play with me, except when I had friends over he'd come in and show off . . . that was embarrassing. I could see the other kids think he was a wally. He wanted me to be interested in rugger and cricket, like him. I did try for ages, but I didn't enjoy it and I wasn't any good at it, so . . .

'He used to pick on me for not being good at sport. It didn't matter what else I was good at, he wasn't interested. Mum was. She used to say I took after her father, and she'd got some of the books he kept, prizes with his name in. She used to take me to museums and interesting places. But that wasn't what he wanted for me. It was the same with her. He always seemed to want what we couldn't give him, and when he couldn't get it, then he said it was our fault, and that we'd let him down. Mum never let him get away with it, though, or I suppose we'd both have ended up nervous wrecks, apologising for our existence. Maybe that would have made him feel better about himself. I don't know. But it would have destroyed us.

'They got to shouting at one another a lot. Or not so much shouting, because Mum doesn't shout. Sort of hissing at one another.

'Then Mum got promotion, and he couldn't go around any longer saying she was "just a silly little woman earning a few pence on the side". That's how he used to refer to her job. I suppose it made him feel better to run her down all the time. He had a good job himself, but he couldn't take it that she was going to be a departmental head.

'I suppose that's what finally did it. There was a terrible row. He said she'd deliberately flouted his orders by taking her car to be serviced at one garage, when he'd told her to take it to another. Stupid. What it was, he needed an excuse, any excuse, to walk out on us. He said it was to give Mum a shock, make her see the error of her ways. So he packed all his best clothes and went to live with this woman he'd met playing badminton. You know, all long legs and not an ounce of fat, bleached fair hair held back with an elastic band.

'All I could think of was what a relief it was to be quiet in the house, to come in and know I wasn't going to be shouted at. Mum cried a bit at first, and said she'd failed. She said she'd tried so hard, but that they didn't seem to talk the same language any more. To tell the truth, I didn't want him back, not even at the beginning. But she talked herself into thinking she ought to try to mend the marriage somehow; go to marriage guidance counselling. She thought maybe he'd been going through a bad patch at work, that perhaps money matters had been troubling him and that her success at work had made him feel inferior. She thought all the usual Christian thoughts about forgiveness and trying again. So she went to see him. Without ringing beforehand.

'Blondie opened the door with a toddler in her arms. Blondie was obviously preggers again. Dad was there, all unbuttoned, watching telly. Home from home. It took a few minutes for Mum to make sense of what she was seeing.

'If it had been me, I reckon I'd have gone for a kitchen knife, but Mum had hysterics, which was probably safer for everyone. Then she got into her car and came home and told me. A couple of days later we had a solicitor's letter saying Dad wanted half the house, so we put it on the market and moved here. The divorce is going through as fast as possible. Mum doesn't want any more of him, and Blondie needs him. It's not so far from our old place, geographically, but everything's different. Mum's OK. She's strong, and she's made herself go out and about. She's coping.

'Me, I reckon I went into shock. I thought I didn't care, but I did. I missed my old friends and the church, and everything. I told myself it would be an adventure to move, that it wasn't going to upset my life. I got involved with Rocco and Kate and you, and I thought I was doing all right. I ought to have known better. I think I'm only just getting over it now.'

That explained a lot about him. I pushed the biscuit tin in his direction, and he helped himself.

He looked at me direct for the first time.

'Sam, I really am sorry. Have I left it too late?'

I said, 'Does Kate know about all this?'

He looked surprised. 'Well, no. I've been rather uptight about it all, and haven't wanted to talk. I'm not used to . . . but I felt you had the right to know. They

76

were worried about you when you stopped coming to the group some weeks ago, and they went on at me to do something about it. I mean, even Rocco volunteered to speak to you about it, but I said no, you wouldn't take it from him.'

Which was probably true.

I said, 'No need to worry about me. I've made up my mind to leave school. You think differently, when you've finished with school. All those petty restrictions, the uniform . . .'

'No uniform in the sixth form.'

'I haven't got there yet. There's exams next year. I haven't a hope of getting good grades.'

'You would, if you got yourself assessed.'

I was going to say 'Thanks, but no thanks!' when Dad came in. Dad has always been quizzy about Luke, and tends to hang around and join in the conversation when he's there.

Dad said, 'Well, what's the news, eh?'

I could see Luke's hand tighten around his mug in self-defence. Luke did not want to talk about himself and the reasons why he'd delayed throwing me a lifeline. Yet I could see him reasoning it out; he'd got to tell Dad or feel he'd failed me and the group, and whatever muddled sense of ethics he'd got in his mind. Or plain Christianity, I suppose.

Whatever.

'Mr Ward, it's like this. We're all very worried about what's been happening to Sam, because everyone knows she's very bright and ought to come out with a bagful of GCSEs. We've found out that if you can get her declared dyslexic by going to a specialist, then Sam can get extra time in the exams, and they'll make some allowances for her problem.'

I could see Dad was going to write Luke off as just another opinionated schoolboy. He put on that condescending, Well, well, what-a-funny-notion, Run-away-and-play look. I couldn't stand that. I trusted Luke to know what he was talking about. A moment before, I'd been all for pooh-poohing the matter, but now I was on Luke's side.

I said, 'I suppose we could look into it.'

Dad's face was a study. He wanted me to be right, but he didn't think a shrimp like Luke could know more than he did about anything.

I said, 'Do you know how to contact this specialist you're talking about, Luke?'

'Er, no. I suppose the school would know.'

I wondered if the school would cooperate, in view of my distinctly dicey record. And did I want them to, anyway? Wouldn't it be better to be free to please myself, and not have to work, work, work? To be myself? Sam Ward, painter and decorator. Or something else physical. Did I really want to go back to all that bitchery at school, competing with Kate and struggling to keep a place in the top set? And it would be a struggle. Could I face Snowcem, knowing how much he hated the sight of me? Was it worth it?

I was inclined to think it wasn't. I wished I'd kept my mouth shut. The parents had been coming round to the idea of my leaving school. What had I let myself in for? Endless aggro, that's what.

Dad was smiling and reaching for the phone. 'I can check this with the Local Authority Education Department at the Town Hall. And if they can't give me a name, perhaps our doctor can. Of course I'll try the school tomorrow, but after the abysmal performance they've put up lately, I'm none too sure they'll be much help.'

You and me both, I thought. I didn't know what to hope for. On balance I hoped they'd leave me in peace.

When I showed Luke out, he put his hand on my shoulder and said, 'See you Sunday, then?'

I shrugged. I was in a mental muddle. I'd gone to the Sunday meetings with very mixed motives. I think I'd mainly gone to be one up on Kate. Now Luke had unbuttoned to me and he hadn't to Kate, so I was definitely one up on her, if not two up.

I wondered why I didn't feel happier about it.

It cost a lot, getting that piece of paper.

The specialist had to be paid for by Mum and Dad, and with Dad on the dole, that was no small problem. We could have gone through the usual Local Education Authority channels I suppose, and maybe got an appointment with some shrink in eighteen month's time. If we were lucky. But we couldn't wait, could we? The parents decided to do it at once, before the end of term, so that I could be officially reinstated etc. At least, that was their hope.

But the specialist was really OK. He had a sallow brown skin, black hair, long thin hands and a pleasant bedside manner. Not that I was in bed, of course.

The parents were seated in his waiting room, and I was taken into his office, where I did all these tests. Most of them you wouldn't recognise as educational tests; at least, I wouldn't. Spacial whatsits, and oral tests and spelling tests and writing tests, and How easily did I learn to tell the time and Did I have any difficulty learning to tie my shoe-laces, for heaven's sake.

I must say, he was thorough. I felt as if he were turning me inside out and looking into all the corners of my brain. He didn't say Ah-ha! when I couldn't do something, and he didn't look especially pleased when I got something right. Somehow he got across the fact that he liked me. I thought that this was something that Luke was going to have to learn about, if he wanted to be a doctor. I wondered what sort of doctor Luke wanted to be.

About half way through that very long morning, the specialist went outside and had a word with the parents to tell them that yes, I was dyslexic and they were not wasting their time in getting me assessed.

His written report made me blush, slightly. 'A girl of Very Superior Intelligence, who could be expected to perform well above the level of her chronological age. She is, however, behind by approximately three and a half years in both spelling and arithmetic.'

He went on to recommend all sorts of aids like a dictionary of Perfect Spelling, and playing Pelmanism.

One of the bits I liked best said that I would benefit from sympathetic teachers, and that a negative reaction to my problem, or a denial that dyslexia exists, would result in frustration or emotional problems!

That made me want to whoop and stand on my head.

Sucks to old Snowcem, and Earl Grey, and all the rest of them!

The dear old doc gave us a piece of paper setting out his report in terms that bureaucrats would understand, asking for special consideration in exams, and all the concessions available to dyslexic pupils.

I can tell you, we walked out on air after that. Even Mum, who had been worrying about the cost of the assessment, looked pleased.

Then it hit me.

I was going to have to go back to school and work.

I did not want to.

Not one bit.

Only, there was no way out. Not after everyone had been to all that trouble. Not after Luke had unburdened himself. And Rocco had been willing to help me. And the parents had put up the money. And all the parents' hopes and fears for me.

I was stuck with it.

Farewell freedom.

Blast. Not just one more year, but three!

Could I stand it?

7

Nothing much happend yesterday.

Dec 17 **LEMAIRE CHANNEL** (cruising)

Weather Cloudy, var winds

*Ship's log: cruised thorugh the narrow Neumayer
Channel in the early monring. Marvellous scenery as
we entered the spectacular and fabled Lemaire Channel,
pushing our way through its ice-strewn narrows in an
attempt to go further south.*

*(Notes: Seen: Wilson Storm petrel, Antarctic tern,
crab eater seals, iceburgs, shags. Humpback whales.*

Southern most point reached   *Lat 65–08 S*
                                  Lon 64 – 04 W

This is as far south as we could get.

I ought to be enjoying this more. I look at everything,
I take part in everything. I have been besotted about this
territory since I was so high. So why can't I be more
relaxed about it?

OK, I'm still getting the nightmare. Shall I try to
describe it? It's nothing much, when you talk about it. I
suppose lots of people get nightmares, and manage to
put them out of their minds during the day. I'm getting
to the point where I dread going to bed, knowing that
I'm going to go through all that horror at about three
o'clock in the morning, and wake up sweating, and
hearing . . .

It is as if the lorry is looming over me all over again,
going flap flap flap . . .

To get back to my story, I returned to school, and if I'd
expected any apology from Snowcem or any of them
well, I ought to have known better. Teachers don't
apologise. They close ranks.

I don't know what they said to one another in their
staff meetings and pastoral care sessions, but they worked
out a formula which suited them, and saved their faces.
The Deputy Head said she understood I was prepared to
take my work more seriously now, and that they were
therefore prepared to give me one more chance, but

would be monitoring my progress carefully.

Which being translated meant that I was shot up back into the top sets for everything, with a mass of home-work to make up on, but that I got more help when I needed it. Mr Toft came back after having been off all that time. He automatically took over the top set again, and I was put back in his class. Really there wasn't anything to be said about the interregnum except to be thankful that it was over. Snowcem disappeared into the woodwork, and we heard later on that he'd taken early retirement . . . though how early that could have been when he was sixty plus in the shade, I don't know.

But all that meant I had no free time at all for watching videos with Rocco, or playing football, and not even much time for cycling around. Boring.

I insisted on keeping on with the Drama Club pro-ductions, and in the holidays I went on Mrs Whittle's theatre workshop and found myself Stage Manager with-out any argument at all. We did some good work that week. The course was held in an amateur but well-equipped theatre in the round. Theatre in the round pres-ents all sorts of problems I hadn't met before. The light-ing board was much more sophisticated for one thing, and I had fun playing around with filters and combi-nations of lights and spots to get different effects. The actors were pretty poor, though.

I went back to the Sunday night group because they made such a point of it, and because in a way I thought I owed it to them. I even asked Kate once if she would like to go with me, but she just shrugged and said she was playing a tennis match. She'd got in with a weird crowd of fifth years, and was rarely seen around with our humble selves. There was a rumour they were into marijuana smoking in the park and drinking, and 'borrowing' cars. I wouldn't have thought it was her scene, really.

But then, I wasn't sure what sort of scene she was moving into. It wasn't that I hankered after her company, exactly. We'd never been that close. It was just that I felt a bit uneasy about the way her life was going.

When I look back on that year I think of hard work, the productions we did in the Drama Club at school, the courses I went on for Mrs Whittle, and not much else. I get flashes of things happening; cycling in Wales which we did as a family holiday after Dad got this last job of his; working a 'spot' for our production of Godspell; watching Luke and Rocco being confirmed at church; cooking a whole lot of pancakes when I was alone in the house one day . . .

I like being alone, to think.

The singlest most interesting thing I did was making the biggest of my toy theatres in wood. It was too big to stand on the shelf, and I had to keep it under my worktop and sit sideways when I did my homework.

I went to church fairly regularly till they started putting the pressure on for me to be confirmed with Luke and Rocco. I'd gone along with almost everything they'd said and done before, because I enjoyed their company after a fashion; it was something to do on a Sunday evening, and some of the things they'd done, like parties, and outings and that . . . they were all right.

But I was no hypocrite, and when it came to the

crunch, I refused to stand up in front of everyone and say I believed when I didn't. Or rather, I did believe in patches. But not enough, and certainly not enough to make a public commitment.

I told them I didn't feel I was ready for it, and they nodded and said that they quite understood. I could feel they were being heavily patient with me. I hate people being patient with me. It's so condescending.

Anyway, after that I sort of drifted off. I got myself on a youth theatre course, and they offered me work experience because they could see I knew what I was doing, handling the lights. And from that I got some professional work in the holidays, backstage at pantos and at large, one-off events. I used to ring up when the holidays were approaching, and they'd say they could use me for a week or three nights or whatever.

That was fun. It's quite true that actors tend to have enormous egos; you never heard such a noise as they made if something upset them. Backstage, we just got on with the job. They were a good crowd backstage. I did a couple more theatre workshops for Mrs Whittle, but found them terribly sloppy and irritating. Mrs Whittle said I'd learned all they had to teach me and it was time for me to move on, which I suppose was about right.

The parents went back into their usual groove after Dad got his new job, and Mum's hours were extended until they were both working full-time. We got a microwave, so that I could do myself some food quickly if I got in before they did.

And so to exam time.

I had my bits of paper, and everyone agreed I was to have extra consideration and all that. I can't remember being excited over the exams or even worried. It was just something I had to get on with. Mum was far more uptight about them than I was, because of wanting me to go on to do accountancy. She said that if I got six passes at C and up, she'd treat me to a mountain bike.

We went on holiday to Greece while we were waiting for the results. I knew it would be OK. I might have messed up one paper but the rest were all right, given the extra time to go over everything properly.

So I got eight subjects, C grades and up.

In a way, I wasn't all that pleased because the parents and the school immediately set higher sights for me. They wanted me to take maths for A levels, and I wanted to do geography and English and history. But they went on at me, both at home and at school, about English and history being too much reading for one with my problems, and so in the end, I agreed.

We were going to choose the mountain bike when they got their new stock in.

Luke and Rocco got through all right, and so – rather to my surprise – did Kate. Not that we spoke much. But I was glad rather than otherwise that I could congratulate her when we met on the street one day just before the start of the new term.

She was still hugging books. Even in the holidays.

I wondered what she'd do now. Presumably she was looking for a job till she got on with her modelling or whatever. So I said, being polite, 'What are you going to do now? Go on the dole?'

'No, I'm staying on. I'm planning to take three As.'

I tried not to look as surprised as I felt.

'Yes, they've all been very encouraging at school, so I thought I'd go for it. The three sciences.'

She was obviously going to try for nursing. I could just see her as a nurse, following the doctors around with those great googly eyes of hers. I tried not to laugh. I said, 'You'll make a very pretty nurse.'

She blushed, I swear she did. 'Well, I know it's hard to get in, but I'm aiming to be a doctor.'

I tried not to laugh, but I just fell about. I tried to pretend I'd got hiccups, but she got the message all right.

'I don't think it's such a silly idea!' she said, reddening. 'But if I don't try, I won't get anywhere. And anyone can daydream, can't they?'

'Sure. I've got the odd daydream, myself.'

'Oh, you. You'll be all right. Probably end up as Chancellor of the Exchequer.'

I tried to change the subject. 'What happened to the boy you were going out with?'

'He's gone to Oxford, studying PPE. I don't suppose I shall see much of him from now on, though he says I'm probably going to have to work harder than him. He's asked me up for a weekend. I'm not sure that I'll go, though. There's an awful lot to do in the sixth form.'

'Sure,' I said, 'and if you don't get to be a doctor, you'll still make a good nurse.' My ribs were still hurting with the desire to laugh, and I wanted to get away round a corner, to explode.

'You really think I don't have what it takes to be a doctor?'

'Well, Kate, I've known you since you were so high, and I can't think of anyone less likely to make a doctor.' It was brutal, of course, but it was best not to let her get the wrong ideas.

She sighed a bit and said, rather wistfully I thought, 'You're always so sure of yourself, Samantha. I wish I were more like you. Luke says . . .'

Ah, now I understood her desire to be a doctor. She wanted to hang on to Luke's coat-tails again.

'. . . I ought to think about it very seriously . . .'

'So you should,' I said, trying not to laugh.

She went off, still hugging her pile of books.

Honestly, I didn't understand why she couldn't think straight about her future. I mean, all she had to do was work out her strengths and her weaknesses, and she'd see where she should be heading.

I was angry with Luke for encouraging her and I went round to tell him so. He and his mother were living in a second floor flat up the road. It was quite nice, all cream walls and pale grey and blue furniture, with a lovely fitted kitchen. She'd gone to town on elaborate curtaining, I suppose because she worked in the shop and could get it at a discount.

Luke's mum is a bit intimidating, with a cool brown stare that starts you wondering if you've got oil from the bike on your face. But she wasn't in when I called round that day.

I said, straight off, 'What's this stupid idea you've got that Kate could study to be a doctor?'

'Hold on,' he said, 'Kate's got the right to try for whatever career she likes.'

'Within reason, yes. But why encourage the poor girl to think she can get into medical school?'

'I don't see why she shouldn't. She got enough GCSEs, her grades were good, and she works hard.'

'Oh, Luke, now you're being stupid! Kate, at medical school? She'd faint at the first drop of blood.'

'She takes splinters out of fingers better than anyone I know.'

'I've never seen her try.'

'You aren't around all that much. Kate has done all her First Aid exams and some voluntary work in the children's ward at the hospital. She's no fool, and she understands what sort of long hours and how much study it entails.'

' "Kate understands?" Are we talking about the same girl?'

He gave me an odd look. 'You've always had a bit of a "down" on her, haven't you?'

'No, I haven't. I just know what she's like, that's all.'

'Well, I think she'll be all right.'

'I hope you know what you're doing. She's likely to give up school altogether when she gets turned down . . .'

'Look who's talking . . .'

I suppose I lost my temper completely, and if I'd given myself time to think, I'd have known that Luke always took the part of the underdog and that I shouldn't have allowed myself to go so far. After I'd cooled down, I did think it extraordinary that Kate had done voluntary work at the hospital and got her First Aid exams.

I had an uneasy feeling that maybe I'd overlooked some good points in the girl.

Of course she'd probably only done it to impress Luke. It was pretty clear to me that since Kate had lost her previous admirer she needed another, and there was Luke, only too anxious to step into the vacant position.

We didn't acknowledge one another's presence in the Common Room on the first day of school, and as I stayed behind to borrow a book, they left school before I did.

I saw them on the pavement together, near the traffic lights. His arm was round her shoulders, and though she was hugging her bag as usual, she was looking up at him in exactly the same way she used to look at her last boy friend, now departed to University.

I jammed on my brakes, and let them get ahead of me. There was quite a lot of traffic on the road, anyway.

I was mad at her. She went from one boy to another, and never cared what harm she did them. Poor Luke.

No, Luke was stupid to let her do that to him. She'd twist him round her little finger, and then go off and . . .

The lights changed and I set off again . . .

And that's when . . .

I can't.

Well. This lorry.

Enormous. Black. Looming. One of those continental ones.

The bike, my bike. I'd had it for years.

A pity about my bike.

Mountain bikes aren't the same, and of course as Dad said, it was a good thing we hadn't actually gone out and bought a new one for me.

I yelled at the driver, I remember that. Only of course he didn't hear me, with his transistor blaring away. I remember hearing the transistor, as I waited at the lights. That sound comes into my nightmare, too.

The canvas sides were done up tightly, neatly, with buck-led straps. Flap flap flap.

The driver didn't indicate that he was turning left. I always looked, and he hadn't. Other people came for-ward afterward to say that he hadn't indicated.

Because he turned that great lorry right across . . . Right across me.

And I could see it coming and coming and . . .

Well, that's the stuff of which nightmares are made, isn't it?

8

Dec 17 **ALMIRANTE BROWN, PARADISE HBR**. *Arr 1330 Dep 1600*

Weather overcast, var winds

Ship's log: We landed at the Argentinian base which is called Almirante Brown. Our first chance to set foot on the Antarctic Peninsula. Then we cruised through the Errera Channle on way to Cuverville Island.

CUVERVILLE ISLAND *Arr 1730 Dep 1930*

Weather overcast, NE winds

Ship's log: Explored the northeastern tip of the island in search of gentoo penguin rookery. Sailed early evening towards the Gerlache Strait where we spotted a number of humpback whales. We followed the wales for a time.

Notes: Seen kelp/Dominican gulls, gentoo, 2 chinstraps, south atlantic skua, Brown skua, leopard seal with krill, iceburgs. Gentoos recognise their mates by sight as well as sound, unlike chinstraps and adelie, who rely on vocal recognition. Gentoos' eyes are the ones best adapted for water.

I suppose I'd better finish this, or I'll never be able to sleep at night again. My cabin mate, Laura, and I talked about it a bit before I went to bed last night. She offered me a sleeping pill, and I was tempted to take it, but I don't really like taking anything, and I don't want to start that sort of thing.

So I got to sleep after a while, and there it was waiting for me in the dark. I never used to *quite* remember what the nightmare was all about. Or not till recently. Not till I began this looking back lark. When I woke up before, I used vaguely to remember something large and threatening looming over me in the nightmare, but I thought it was a person. My first teacher? The one who used to shout at me all the time?

Maybe nightmares change, over the years. I think I did used to have nightmares about her when I was little. That's when Mum got me the night lamp and the stuffed penguin. That's odd. I'd forgotten that's when she got me the penguin.

Then for years there were no nightmares. I had nasty dreams while I was in hospital, but I thought that was the drugs they'd given me. Those dreams were mostly about the lorry, but not always. It's understandable I dreamed about the lorry, then, but it's two years since the accident, and I thought I'd got it out of my system. Why should it surface now?

The great big, giant-size traffic lights . . . the sound of the tranny, only much louder . . . the loom of the lorry over me . . . the flap flap flap of its sides . . . and me screaming my head off . . .

Nowadays when I wake up sweating, I check that I'm not still under the lorry, and that I can actually move my legs and arms.

I used to find the movement of the ship soothing, but last night as I went off to sleep, it felt as though I was being pushed around on a hospital trolley. I was unconscious when they took me to hospital, of course. And for days afterwards.

I don't remember anything about that bit. Four days of nothing, they told me, afterwards.

It was a bit like drowning. You went down and down and there was nothing, and then you were vaguely aware of being uncomfortable and distant voices and then more drowning. And up again, and being sharply uncomfortable and more voices and deciding you didn't want to know and going down again.

Up and down for a while. And then everything got decidedly unpleasant.

I'll skip that bit.

Honestly, Mum's face is a dead give-away, and as a liar she is not in the championship category, so I knew something was very wrong, the first time I woke up and recognised her sitting by my bed. But I couldn't cope with it for a while.

Even when I overheard one of the nurses saying something about me to another of the nurses, I didn't take it in. Didn't want to take it in.

'. . . shouldn't she be going to Stoke Mande . . . ?'

Stoke. Stoke. Stoke Mandeville.

The words 'Stoke Mandeville' hovered around in my head, and I knew I could make something of them if I tried, but I didn't want to try.

The words went on clicking through my head. Stoke Mandeville was the place you went to if you'd damaged yourself pretty well beyond repair. Wheelchairs. Tetraplegics.

I didn't know what a 'tetraplegic' was, but it sounded pretty duff to me.

I was visited by my parents, of course, and by Luke and Rocco and Kate and some of the Sunday night group. They came and went and were all very cheerful and looked at me with identical expressions. Sort of falsely bright and cheerful.

I knew with one level of my mind what that look meant, and what the nurse had meant, but I wasn't going to be tidied away into a wheelchair. I was going to get well, and walk out of there before they could say 'Stoke Mandeville' to my face.

'Well, darling,' my mother said, 'I expect you're right, but you have got a lot of broken bones, you know. Pelvis, ribs, leg. And concussion. It's going to take ages.'

'I'll be on my feet in no time,' I said.

She gaped at me, lines of worry deepening. I knew then that they weren't sure if I'd ever walk again. She didn't admit it, of course. She didn't know how to cope, so she started crying and went off to fetch Sister, and Sister tried to shush me and told me not to get excited.

'I'm not excited,' I said. 'I'm just bored. I'm not going to have hysterics if I hear the truth. I just want to know what I have to do to get out of here.'

She blinked a bit and put on one of those rat-trap mouths that means its owner is not going to talk, no matter how much you torture them. A lot of the nurses were like that. I suppose they were under instructions not to depress me by saying how unlikely it was that I ever would get out of there on my own two feet.

Idiots.

If I'd got through school so far with all my problems, then I could beat this one, too.

Luke said they were all praying for me.

Fat lot of use that was, I thought. But I didn't say so. Maybe it did do some good. After all, it never even entered my head to give in. Perhaps positive thinking – and prayer is positive thinking, isn't it? – perhaps that helped. It helped Mum and Dad to keep sane, anyway. They'd never been so regular at church before.

I asked for my school books, but they'd got swept away in the general chaos after the accident, as had my school bag. I was livid when I found out about the bike. I really liked that bike.

It was Kate who talked to me about the future. It's odd, that. You'd have thought she'd have been the first to duck reality, but she didn't. She asked me to talk about how I felt. No-one else did. They all wanted to stop me as soon as I tried to talk about the future. Which only made it clear to me that they didn't think I had a future.

Kate said, 'I found out that you can have a tutor for your A levels, here in hospital. And I got you some more books and some notepads from school. Mr Toft says he'll set you work, if you can cope with it. OK?'

Very much OK. My right arm still worked, although I couldn't write for long because of the way it had been wrenched about. The left was less cut about, but my writing was even more scrawly with my left than with my right, so we decided to keep going on the right.

Geography was OK. They found me really nice tutors, who came in and taught me. Also Mr Toft kept popping in after school to bring me books and that . . . a welcome change from the moans and groans of the geriatrics into whose midst I was dumped after the first week or two.

They couldn't find me a tutor for maths. It should have been easier to find one for maths than for geography, but first they tried to contact this person and then that, and what with them taking holidays and bereavements and so on, I was left dangling. I tried to keep on working at it, and Kate got me work from school, but somehow it just didn't work out.

I could cope with the English and the geography all right, but after half an hour of maths, I had such a headache that I had to give up. Mum got upset about that, because it was 'her' subject and going to lead on to my doing accountancy, but the hospital said I shouldn't push it, because of the concussion I'd suffered.

Then they found out it wouldn't count against my doing accountancy if I'd got a good GCSE and two other As. So I let maths slide.

And believe me, two A levels are enough to be going on with, if you're flat on your back in hospital and doped to the eyeballs for the pain.

Kate brought me a Walkman and borrowed cassettes from the library for me. I thought about learning Spanish by cassette, and did a bit but not enough to take it up. It was all rather infantile, Costa Bella holiday stuff. Not really interesting enough to take seriously.

When my pelvis and leg had mended enough, I got going on crutches. Hard work, but it's better to be vertical than horizontal. The physios were helpful. Kate said she'd never be able to do their job, and perhaps she'd better go in for dentistry instead. I think she meant it to be a joke, but she doesn't usually make jokes, so I'm not sure about that. Funnily enough, I *was* beginning to see her as some kind of medic. She had that detached look you get with the best specialists. (Not that she'll ever be a specialist, of course!)

I was out of the hospital and walking on elbow crutches by Christmas, and back at school in January. The hospital gave me some sticks to walk with, but I threw them away on my first day back at school. Dad gave me a lift to school, and I took a taxi back.

After I went home, Dad told me that the doctors had said I would never walk again, that there was probably permanent brain damage, and that I could well have ended up as a vegetable.

I don't know why people in hospitals don't take into consideration the type of person you are. They say that they do, but they don't. I remember Sister looked really alarmed when she first saw me hoist myself to my feet. She said it was too early.

She was wrong.

I knew my bones would knit well. I'm fair skinned, so the various places where they'd stitched me up all healed well. I'm lucky that way.

I had had to drop one A level, but that was all right by me. I could still get a place to do accountancy, and Dad sued the pants off the firm that owned the lorry, and once their advisers had seen my X rays, they paid up.

So, the occasional taxi was all right.

That's how I came to be on this voyage. I couldn't ever have afforded it, otherwise. Dad put most of the money aside for me, but said I could go on this trip if I got good A levels.

I'm eighteen, now. I got my A levels with respectable grades. I've got a place to study accountancy, starting in January. The fact that I'm bored with maths is neither here nor there. I suppose that's part of growing up, facing the fact that you're bored with your life's work.

Everything in the garden's lovely.

So why do I still get nightmares?

Dec 18 **ANTARCTIC SOUND** (*cruising*)

Weather cloudy, var winds

Ship's log: We squeezed our way through the ice field of the Antarctic Sound in an attempt to reach the Weddell Sea, but failed. We did some zodiac cruising off Rosamel Island instead.

Notes: I saw leopard seals, crabeater seals and a number of adelie penguins. Went to barbecue on the pooldeck with huge tabular iceburgs as backdrop. No landing possible due to pack ice. Seen starboard at lunch, young killer whale (orca). Saw white Giant petrel, snow petrel, pintato, antarctic tern, melt waterfall, shags, adelie, young penguins on iceburgs, crabeater seal, iceburg tipping over, kelp, gull.
Lecture: 'Copacabana: An Antarctic Field Station.'

We weren't that far away when the berg tipped over. It went so slowly at first, I wasn't sure it was really moving. Then it tipped over and the sea swelled out around it. The bottom – that's the bit that's now on top – is all jagged and quite unlike the part of the berg which had been on top. The colours were dense blue and grey.

I am trying to be subjective about this, but when that berg began to tip over, I got a giddy feeling. In my ears

I could hear that awful tinny music from the transistor in the cab of the lorry.

I shut my eyes, and held my breath. I only opened my eyes again when the iceberg was dipping into the water and the sea surged out around it.

Big things, all sorts of big things, do that to me now-adays. Like those awful leopard seals. But the way that iceberg tipped, so slowly, so inevitably . . . I wanted to scream, but couldn't.

Laura saw I was upset and though she didn't know why, she was nice about it. She brought me down into our cabin and sat me down and asked if I wanted a drink. I don't have that much money to spend on mess bills, so I said I was all right.

She's really nice. She said she'd overheard bits of this recording that I've been doing, and she asked if it was something to do with Kate, and I said absolutely not.

Then my head started spinning again, and I said I'd lie down for a bit, and she went away. It was because I'd been having so many broken nights, of course. Things kept spinning and spinning . . . the iceberg toppling intercut with the lorry toppling . . . and the sound of the transistor tinnily coming through the cab door and the chuff chuff of the air brakes as the driver tried to inch forward at the lights . . .

Penguins en masse make a terrible sound. Quite deafening. Squawk squawk, chuff chuff. The seal lunged forward to grab the penguin and we couldn't do anything but watch, and I'll never forget that, not to my dying day.

Kate's head in a nimbus of light, as she sat by my bed

in the hospital.

I hate her.

Always have.

She gets everything and I get nothing. She's got her four As and is going on to train to be a doctor, and I suppose she'll be perfect at that as she's always been perfect at everything, ever since I've known her.

Luke, now. He's aiming to be a surgeon. He's going to a different University from Kate. They are not going out together. That was all in my imagination.

Or was it? I've got to face the fact that I did want to keep them apart, though I hadn't any right to do so. I'm not in love with Luke. I'm not in love with anyone. It was all to spite Kate. I am not a very nice person.

I Am Not Going To Go To Sleep.

I'm going up on deck again. I'll walk around all night, if I have to.

9

Dec 19 LION'S RUMP, KING GEORGE ISL.
Arr0730 Dep 1130

Weather cloudy, var winds

*Ship's log: We explored the adelie penguin rookery.
Elephant seals live there, too. 2 members of the party
left the ship to join one of the settlements here at
Copacabana in Admiralty Bay for their research work.
On to Maxell Bay.*

I don't like seeing the seals so close to the penguins any
more. I'm worn out. I can hardly think straight. I took
one of Laura's sleeping pills last night so I blacked out
for a while, but now I'm only half awake, and have

missed really experiencing the thrill of seeing so many adelie penguins close to.

I'm like the penguins.

No, I didn't mean that. I mean, I like penguins.

Why did I say I was like the penguins? Har, har. Stupid Sam strikes again. Fancy calling myself a penguin. Put it down to having too little sleep.

Of course I am clumsy sometimes, like the penguins. I wonder why God made them like that? They clown about just like I do sometimes, when I'm trying to make other people laugh.

But I'm not like them in other ways. I mean, I can't slide into the sea and shear through the water and tumble and dive and swoop as they do. I don't have that equivalent in my life.

Well, the theatre work, I suppose.

If that counts.

I mean, if I were a different sort of person, I could make the theatre my life. Study stage management. I've done all those extra courses in the holidays and helped with professional theatre staging, and done all the productions at school for yonks. I suppose I could get a job in the theatre?

I'm being daft. The parents would go bananas.

Accountancy is so safe.

Accountancy is boring. I am bored with the very idea of it.

Some girl on the last theatre course I attended was going to get a place to study stage management at the Bristol Old Vic. I suppose I could . . .

No.

Get back to reality, girl. That sort of thing is not for you. You have got to be practical, to face facts. Do what you're cut out for.

The theatre.

Let's take it slowly, one word at a time.

I *am* bored with the idea of doing accountancy. OK. So what else am I fit for?

The theatre.

I'd be a fish out of water – a penguin out of water – if I went in for accountancy. I'd always be clowning about, and being jealous of people and trying to go one better. Like I did with Kate. I did try to put her down. I haven't been very nice to her. How she put up with me, I don't know. I'm glad she got through to medical school. If she wants to go out with Luke, then she shall. I don't have to have Luke for my special friend. I make friends easily in the theatre. Backstage, of course.

If God made me, then he meant there to be a special place where I could be myself. The place he intended me to find. Perhaps that's why I've had such a rough ride. Every time I try to be like Kate, or try to go one better than her, I fall flat on my face.

When I get back, maybe I could tell the parents how I feel about the theatre and accountancy. Maybe they'll help me and maybe they won't, but I suppose I know which way I ought to be going now.

One thing I could do, definitely and without any 'maybes': I could go to see Kate and tell her I'm sorry. And Luke, too. I haven't been a good friend to either of them, though they've stuck by me, I can't think why.

Luke told me just before I came away that I had to

look within myself and come to terms with what I found. You can't be out here in this great white, clean world, unmarked by human mistakes, and not want to be clean, too. I'm not particularly clean. I wish I were.

Dear God, can you hear me? If you can, then please, I'm sorry. I've been stupid and mean and jealous and honestly, I wonder why you put up with me. When I get back, I'm going to do my best to set things right, and I'm going to go back to the Sunday night group and learn all I can and try all I can to be better. Please help me to do better. I thought I could do it all myself, but I can't. I've denied you exist. When I was in hospital, I thought I was doing it all by myself, but really it was you answering other people's prayers. I am ashamed, I really am. And I will try to do better.

Dec 19 TENIENTE. MARSH/ BELLINGHAUSEN *arr 1630Dep 2200*

Weather overcast, var winds

Ship's log: Guided tour to the Chilean base Teniente Marsh and to the Russian Base Bellinghausen. People from both bases came on board for dinner. The crew put on a colourful show as we left Admiralty Bay. (Guess what! I knew all the songs they sang from working in the theatre!) This was to be our last sight of the White Continent as we went through the Nelson Strait.

Notes: And a good time was had by all. I swopped

patches and pins for pins, photos and postcards. All with the comment, Sorry, I've no dollars. Net result 10 USSR pins, all diferent, and a similar no of photos in exchange for 4 patches, 5 pins and a T-shirt.

I slept without a nightmare last night. Laura and I had a long talk. She's been great. She's been listening to my tapes and she said she was no trained psychiatrist, but she thought I was at a crossroads in my life, and that this had put me under stress. All the fears which I had repressed – of failure, of the lorry – then came up and hit me in my nightmares. It's a funny thing, but I remember now that I did use to have nightmares when I was a child, and they were all about that first awful teacher of mine.

When I told Laura how I felt about the penguins, she fetched out her Bible and showed me this:

The Lord said:
'How fast the wings of an ostrich beat!
But no ostrich can fly like a stork.
The ostrich leaves her eggs on the ground
for the heat in the soil to warm them.
She is unaware that a foot may crush them
or a wild animal break them.
She acts as if the eggs were not hers,
and is unconcerned that her efforts were wasted.
It is I who made her foolish
and did not give her wisdom.
But when she begins to run,

she can laugh at any horse or rider.'

It's the same with the penguins. On land they look daft, but in their right place, they're supreme. I'd never read anything from the Book of Job before. I thought it was all breast-beating and dreary. Laura lent me her Bible, and I learned the bit about the ostrich by heart.

Dec 20 **DRAKE PASSAGE** (*cruising*)

Weather: overcast/fog, NW winds

Ship's log: moderate sea and swell on northwestward way to the Drake Passage. Bird-watching, lectures. Lecture: 'The world of the whale. Lecture by Dr. Gerhard Reimer, 'Fauna and Flora of Patagonia' (in German: I didn't go.) Lecture: 'Plate Tectonics – Commotion under the Ocean.'

Practically everyone went to bed early because tomorrow we're rounding Cape Horn, and they want to be fresh for that. I stood on the Obs desk all by myself, and quoted from the Book of Job.

'. . . and God said: Who are you to question my wisdom with your ignorant, empty words? Stand up now like a man and answer the questions I ask you. Were you there when I made the world? Have you ever in all your life commanded a day to dawn? Have you been to the springs in the depths of the sea? Has anyone ever shown you the gates that guard the dark world of the dead? . . . I know, Lord, that you are all-powerful; that you can do everything you want. You ask how I dare question your wisdom when I am so very ignorant. I am ashamed of all I have said . . .'

Dec 21 **CAPE HORN,** *Chile Arr 1500 Dep 1830*

Weather cloudy/overcast, NW winds

Ship's log: rounded Cape Horn before heading to Caleta Leon, the sheltered cove at the SE tip of Horn Island. Landed and climbed a wooden staircase and explored the dense tussock of the island. Had a great view of the bottom of the South American Continent.

Notes: Saw some magallanic (Jackass) penguins after a muddy walk through the breast-high tussock gras. Also saw lots of kelp which grows a foot or more each day. Also an otter on the cliffs from the zodiac. Signed the visitors book.

At 1830H, weighed anchor and headed towards Beagle Channel.

I'm rounding Cape Horn, tarantara!

Dec 22 **PUERTO WILLIAMS**

Ship's log: Docked alongside naval wharf at 0600 hrs.

They gave me two certificates.

1. *Certificate of Antarctic Discoverers, signed by the expedition leaders. 'Samantha Ward has joined the ranks of Scott and Shackleton, and ventured to set foot upon Antarctica, the highest, coldest, driest, windiest, loneliest, most remote and least known continent on earth.'*

2. *'Certificate of Landing as a conqueror of the notorious Cape Horn. Samantha Ward has accomplished a feat of which few sailors can boast: to stand at the very end of the earth and look at one time upon the Atlantic Ocean, the Pacific Ocean and the Drake Passage.' Signed by the expedition leaders.*

I'm going to be all right, now.

Some more books in the *Impressions* series
For the Love of Money   **Trevor Ross**

Baz and Nick raid the council office safe and at first congratulate themselves on a successful job. But their getaway has been spotted by Nick's brother, Damian, who is torn between loyalty to his brother and guilt at an innocent man being accused of the crime. The suspect is a member of the beach mission team and tension rises as he is arrested.

'But you haven't told the best bit, Liz,' broke in Jenny, as she took up the story. 'When we arrived back at Green Shutters from the beach there was another police car outside and a constable guarding the door!'

'Not only that, there were two detectives inside, ransacking the whole house,' added Liz.

'That's right!' said Jenny, enjoying herself again. 'Kate had to let them in – she was the only one left in this afternoon. They went through all our bedrooms, obviously looking for the stolen money. And they kept us in the garden for half an hour before they let us in!'

'Did they find anything?' said Damian, though he already knew the answer to that one.

'No,' said Liz, 'which is probably why they released him.'

'You mean they haven't kept him under lock and key in their cells, and fed him on bread and water?' Al sounded disappointed and Jenny giggled, elbowing him in the ribs.

Liz ignored them. 'No they let him go this evening, but gave Tim strict instructions that he was to be responsible for him and that Graham mustn't leave Shelham.'

'So he's in the clear.' Damian felt very relieved, though the others could not have guessed how much.

'Not quite. You see, they've matched Graham's fingerprints with the ones on the office telephone,' Liz ended, and for once Jenny and Al had nothing funny to say.

Rat Pack   Mollie Thompson

Gail and her Rat Pack are well known for their bullying
tactics. When Rachel stands up for herself Gail is so
furious that she plans her revenge with no thought for
the consequences. She discovers that followers can be
fickle as the Rat Pack melts away.

All week Rachel had been keeping well out of Gail's
way, but by Thursday she knew that she couldn't
do so any longer. This was the day when Gail was
expecting that essay to be supplied. Rachel had kept
her resolve and had not written a single word on
the sheaf of file paper that Gail had previously
insisted on giving her. But now that the time for
returning it was close Rachel began to feel very
nervous. Gail would certainly not appreciate blank
sheets of paper.

Wayne was standing over by the window talking
with some of his pals but he'd been watching for
Gail's arrival, and as she walked in through the
doorway Wayne very casually sauntered across the
room.

Although her mouth was dry and her knees felt
a bit wobbly Rachel realised that her moment had
come, and she felt very reassured to know that
Wayne was there. he'd said he'd be right behind
her and indeed he was . . . three feet behind her.
That fact alone gave her the confidence and the
courage she needed.

Rachel looked Gail straight in the eyes, thrust
the empty sheets of paper at her and shook her

head.

'I haven't written anything for you.'

There were gasps of amazement and disbelief from some Rat Packers nearby, and a shocked silence from everyone else. Gail's face was a study in bulging anger: her face changed colour from pasty white to furious red and her eyes narrowed.

'What did you say?' she said with slow deliberation.

Rachel still held the white sheets of paper stiffly in front of her.

'I said I haven't written your homework essay for you.'

'And why not?'

'Because it isn't right: it's cheating.'

A murmur of whispered comment greeted that last statement but it wasn't immediately obvious if they were agreeing with Rachel or supporting Gail.

'But you promised. We had a contract and now you've broken it.' Gail, with her usual flair for drama, had taken on the role of an American gangster and was busily inventing the plot as she went along. 'You know what happens to people who welsh on a deal? Well, I'll tell you, they get a "contract" taken out on *them*.'

There was a ripple of laughter from the Rat Pack who'd probably heard Gail playing her gangster role on other occasions. But for Rachel there was nothing but menace in Gail's remark. However, there was nothing to be gained from looking scared. Now that she'd set off on this course of action she decided that she might as well say what she really thought, regardless of the consequences.

Love and Laura   **Audrey Hopkins**

A writing assignment for the summer holidays? Laura
jumps at the chance because she wants to be a writer.
She chooses love as her subject and remembers the times
in her life when love has been all important.

Then she meets David and, through their friendship
the project merges with what is happening now.

'This is special, Gran. Mr Carter thinks I'm good
at writing so I'm going to work at it all holiday.
The only trouble is . . . I don't know what to write
about.'

'That's a good start! You're always telling me
about school and the youth club at church and
Debbie's always around full of ideas,' she went on,
pouring herself another cup.

'Debbie's going to Kenya. Everybody's off to
foreign parts so I won't be doing much at all,' I
said as I cleared my things and ran some hot water
into the sink.

'That was a good pot of tea,' Gran said as she
drained her cup and passed it to me. 'I do love a
good cuppa.'

I washed the two cups and the plate, then followed her into the shop, my thoughts still on holidays.

'I'd love to go to Kenya,' I sighed. 'Debbie is so
lucky. Do you know she went ski-ing at Easter –
to the USA! Can I have a marshmallow?'

Gran nodded and popped four of the pink and
white mallows into a bag for me.

'I love marshmallows,' I said, biting into a pink one. 'And I love you, Gran.'

'So, you love marshmallows and Kenya and me . . . in that order?'

I laughed. 'You're top of the list, Gran. It's a funny word, isn't it?'

'What? Marshmallow?'

'No, *love*. It can mean so many things.'

A customer came in then so I went back up to my room and changed to go shopping. I always do the Saturday shopping when Mum has been on the Friday night shift. There is a big open market in town and the fruit and vegetables are really fresh and cheap. Mum had left the shopping money on the sideboard with a list so I put that in my bag along with my own purse. I had managed to save a few pounds from the money Gran gives me for helping in the shop and by cutting down on lunch at school. There is a stall in the market that sells second-hand clothes, really good quality stuff too. The girl who runs it has an eye for fashion and I've had designer clothes for less than five pounds! She saw me coming and waved something in russet brown and gold over her head.

'I've been saving these for you,' she called. 'Your size and colour . . . are you interested?'

Was I interested? Cotton culottes like the ones she was waving cost thirty pounds in the shops!

'I love them,' I said. 'How much?'

My heart sank when she answered. Eight pounds! I had five but she wouldn't take any less. I had Mum's money on me but I couldn't use that so I had to walk away. I was still feeling angry and miserable when I bumped into Lisa.

'I'm shopping for my holiday,' she said. 'Come with me.'

Walking Disaster   Gail Vinall

Mel is stunned when she is not selected for the school team for the annual Ten Tors hike. She cannot believe that the reason is because she lacks team spirit.

Mel joins the church youth club team instead, feeling she is doing them a favour but on the hike she is in for some surprises.

'Where's your new curate?' Mel asked. 'I've got to see him.' She had almost forgotten the real reason for coming along.

'I don't think he can make it tonight. Another meeting or something.'

'Drat! Oh well, you'll do. Are there still vacancies for the Ten Tors team?'

'Yes. Why, have you got someone in mind?'

'Myself, actually.'

'You! Crikey, that'd be brilliant. Wait till I tell the others. We were getting worried we'd have to drop out. Hang on there.'

Mel watched him dart away with a very satisfied feeling. She was needed and wanted once more. This could turn out even better than the school team. There, she was just one of the gang; here, she would be special, superior, looked up to.

'Here they are, the team,' Mike announced proudly. 'Meet Mel.'

The smile faded on Mel's lips. What a motley crew they looked. Two insipid-looking girls with mousy hair giggled behind their hands. The taller girl had fine hair, cut in a bob, a wide mouth and hundreds of freckles. Her friend had long hair tied up in a dumb pony-tail which accentuated her broad face and the fact that she was easily a stone overweight. A tall, morose-looking boy with spots shuffled uneasily in the background and another smaller lad with spiky brown hair peered at her through round glasses. His ears stuck out.

If Mel had ever made a mistake it was now. Call this a team? Apart from Mike there wasn't one who looked as if they'd know how to navigate to the crossroads let alone across Dartmoor. Was it too late to back out?

'Here's a copy of our training schedule,' Mike said, handing her a blue sheet. 'We start this week-end, meeting here after school on Friday. Just a fifteen miler, with one night camping.'

What had she done? Fancy spending a precious weekend with this lot!

Hidden Prizes   Audrey Constant

Paula is starting a promising career in show jumping. But there are rival priorities – her family need her help on the farm and she wants to organise riding sessions for disabled children. Paula has to make some hard decisions.

Bruce put down the letters he was reading. 'I don't understand you,' he said. 'You're ambitious and I've given you this job with plenty of opportunities. I believe you've got a great future ahead of you and there aren't many I can say that about. Now you're thinking of exchanging all that for some whim you've thought up. If you're going to get anywhere in this game, you've got to be single-minded, to the exclusion of everything else. It's tough, but it's the only way.'

'But if I organise a few sessions for those children in my own time and at our place, why shouldn't I? I promise you that it won't affect my work in any way. I'm just as keen as ever I was to do well and I'm grateful to you for offering me the job. You know that, Bruce.'

He relented a little. 'Then just remember to keep it that way. I'm not interested in charitable institutions. There's no room for that in my life and I think that if you're to do your job properly, you won't have time either. You have no idea of the work involved in something like that. It's not my business what you do in your time off, but if you go ahead with this, it seems inevitable that you won't be giving your whole mind and energy to what we're doing here. I'm just warning you, that's all. I don't want to hear any more about it.'

It was no good arguing. Everyone was against it. They were only to willing to point out the difficulties and the annoying part was that they were right a lot of the time. Even Matthew had warned me.

Perhaps, I thought, I should give up the idea. I didn't want to risk things going wrong because I went ahead against advice. I was determined then to put it firmly out of my mind. But it wasn't that easy. It kept creeping back. I even prayed about it. I asked God to make it clear to me, one way or the other, what he thought I ought to do. Perhaps I didn't have enough faith because there was no direct answer, and I can't say I expected one.

Then two things happened to prove me wrong.